LEARNING TO
LEAD
AS A DISCIPLE
OF JESUS

PHILIPPIANS

BRENT CROWE

Lifeway Press®
Nashville, Tennessee

Editorial Team

Kyle Wiltshire
Content Editor

Morgan Hawk
Production Editor

Jon Rodda
Art Director

Karen Daniel
Editorial Team Leader

John Paul Basham
Manager, Student Ministry Publishing

Ben Trueblood
Director, Student Ministry

Published by Lifeway Press® • © 2021 Brent Crowe

No part of this book may be reproduced or transmitted in any form or by any means, electronic or mechanical, including photocopying and recording, or by any information storage or retrieval system, except as may be expressly permitted in writing by the publisher. Requests for permission should be addressed in writing to Lifeway Press®; One Lifeway Plaza; Nashville, TN 37234.

ISBN 978-1-0877-4781-1 • Item 005833143

Dewey decimal classification: 227.6
Subject headings: RELIGION / Christian Ministry / Youth

Unless otherwise noted, all Scripture quotations are taken from the Christian Standard Bible®, Copyright © 2017 by Holman Bible Publishers. Used by permission. Christian Standard Bible® and CSB® are federally registered trademarks of Holman Bible Publishers.

Scripture quotations from THE MESSAGE. Copyright © by Eugene H. Peterson 1993, 1994, 1995, 1996, 2000, 2001, 2002. Used by permission of NavPress. All rights reserved. Represented by Tyndale House Publishers, Inc.

To order additional copies of this resource, write to Lifeway Resources Customer Service; One Lifeway Plaza; Nashville, TN 37234; fax 615-251-5933; phone toll free 800-458-2772; order online at lifeway.com; or email orderentry@lifeway.com.

Printed in the United States of America

Student Ministry Publishing • Lifeway Resources
One Lifeway Plaza • Nashville, TN 37234

CONTENTS

About the Author 4
Introduction 5

SESSION 1
The Art of Initiative and Gratitude 6

SESSION 2
The Excellent, Bold, Optimistic Leader 20

SESSION 3
Humility 34

SESSION 4
Countercultural Success 48

SESSION 5
Empowerment 62

SESSION 6
The Myth of Confidence 76

SESSION 7
An Ethic of Thinking Well 90

Leader Guide 104

ABOUT THE AUTHOR

Brent Crowe is a thought-provoking visionary and communicator who has a passion to present the life-changing message of the gospel. Brent uses humor and real-life situations to relate to people at the heart of their struggles. The roles of husband, father, minister, evangelist, author, and leader have allowed Brent to influence people from all walks of life throughout his twenty years in ministry.

Engaging issues such as leadership, culture, and change, Brent speaks to hundreds of thousands across the nation and abroad each year and is currently serving as Vice President for Student Leadership University, a program that has trained over one hundred and fifty thousand students to commit themselves to excellence.

He is also the author of *Moments 'til Midnight, Sacred Intent: Maximize the Moments of Your Life, Reimagine: What the World Would Look Like If God Got His Way, Chasing Elephants: Wrestling with the Gray Areas of Life,* the Associate Editor of *IMPACT: The Student Leadership Bible,* and the co-author of *The Call.* His latest work will be released in November 2021.

The desire of Brent's heart is to see people realize that they have been set apart to the gospel of God, and in turn, they must set their lives apart in an effort to capture every moment in worshipful service to Him.

Brent Crowe is married to Christina and has six children, Gabe, Charis, Za'Riah, Mercy, Zi'Yon, and Aryanna. He holds a Doctorate in Philosophy and two masters degrees, a Masters of Divinity in Evangelism and a Masters of Arts in Ethics, from Southeastern Baptist Theological Seminary.

INTRODUCTION

How do you lead, influence, and shine in the world today? Many people toil tirelessly trying to build their own personal brand, faking it until they make it. But as a disciple of Jesus, how should you approach leadership, influence, and shining for all to see? What should direct your path and guide your thoughts?

In Paul's letter to the Philippians, he offers a guide for our quest. To sum it up succinctly, leadership begins at the feet of Jesus. Paul knew this all too well. For a long time, he tried really hard to do it his way—and then Jesus. We really can stop there because that's what Jesus did on a dusty road to Damascus. He stopped Paul, then called Saul, dead in his tracks.

That's what this Bible study is all about, helping you learn how to lead like Jesus. Thankfully, it's not some aspirational, unattainable, distant star you can never reach. Leading like Jesus is simple, but costly. It means considering others, living in gratitude, serving with humility, embracing boldness, striving for excellence, and a divine optimism that can only come from Jesus Himself. It's countercultural and takes initiative, but it's worth it. I'm excited for you to take this journey and I look forward to seeing how Jesus will teach you to shine like stars in the world!

HOW TO USE

VIDEO GUIDE: Begin each session by watching the video of Brent's teaching and interviews. There is a Video Guide at the start of each session to help students follow along while watching.

GROUP DISCUSSION: Every session includes a Group Discussion to help lead students through the material, either on their own or as a group. Be sure to save time to answer the discussion questions at the end of each session.

PERSONAL STUDY: Each session also includes four days of personal study. Encourage students to set aside time throughout the week leading up to your next group meeting to complete these pages.

LEADER GUIDE: In the back of this study, there is a Leader Guide to help leaders prepare for each session with an outline, Scripture references, optional applications, and prayer prompts.

SESSION 1

THE ART OF INITIATIVE AND GRATITUDE

Session 1

VIDEO GUIDE

SCRIPTURE:

I give thanks to my God for every remembrance of you, always praying with joy for all of you in my every prayer, because of your partnership in the gospel from the first day until now. I am sure of this, that he who started a good work in you will carry it on to completion until the day of Christ Jesus. Indeed, it is right for me to think this way about all of you, because I have you in my heart ...
PHILIPPIANS 1:3-7a

NOTES:

INTERESTING QUOTE:

KEY POINTS:

Larry Takes Flight

In 1982, at the age of thirty-three, a truck driver named Larry Walters was sitting in his backyard in Los Angeles, California. Leaning back in a lawn chair with a cool beverage in hand and a nice breeze on his face, a thought entered his mind, "I wonder what it would be like to fly?" It was a thought that had been with him since childhood. No one quite knows why this moment was different from all the others, but what happened next caught the attention of the world.

Larry acquired forty-five helium weather balloons, a two-way radio, a parachute, some sandwiches, and a BB gun.[1] The idea was to attach the balloons to the lawn chair, float up above his neighborhood, enjoy a simple meal, maybe talk to someone on the radio, then systematically shoot the balloons until he safely—and slowly—descended back to the ground below. What could possibly go wrong? (Don't try this at home—things go wrong.)

Once Larry began floating up in his flying lawn chair, he just kept on going higher and higher. The next thing he knew, he was two miles above the earth's surface and hovering in the airspace of Los Angeles International Airport. Planes on approach that day looked out their window and struggled to believe what they were seeing: a man with a BB gun floating in a lawn chair! As the balloons began to lose their helium, Larry rapidly came crashing back to earth and landed in power lines, which most likely saved his life.

Larry survived his flight, though he was hospitalized for a while. Eventually, he got back to normal life, and everyone wanted to interview him. Robert Fulghum wrote about Larry's flight in his classic work *All I Really Need to Know I Learned in Kindergarten*. He pointed out that all the journalists and television talk show hosts who interviewed Larry asked the same basic questions:

"Were you scared?"

"Why did you do it?"

Each time Larry gave the same response, "Was I scared? Wonderfully so." As to the why, he would simply say, "You can't just sit there."[2]

TAKING INITIATIVE

So much of leadership is about coming to that place in our lives where we think, "I'm not just sitting here anymore!" Our leadership journey doesn't just happen. Instead, it begins when we take initiative. Initiative is a willingness to take an active role in our lives to learn to lead as disciples of Jesus. That's right, leadership isn't something separate from being a disciple, nor do the terms mean the same thing. Rather, as disciples of Jesus, we must learn to cultivate and steward our influence. For disciples who want to influence for the glory of God, leadership begins at the feet of Jesus.

Describe a time in your life when you felt like you couldn't just sit there anymore and you took the initiative to lead.

Paul is one of the greatest examples of a leader in the world and in church history. He provided a starting point for our discussion in the opening words of his letter to the Philippians:

> *I give thanks to my God for every remembrance of you, always praying with joy for all of you in my every prayer, because of your partnership in the gospel from the first day until now. I am sure of this, that he who started a good work in you will carry it on to completion until the day of Christ Jesus. Indeed, it is right for me to think this way about all of you, because I have you in my heart, and you are all partners with me in grace, both in my imprisonment and in the defense and confirmation of the gospel. For God is my witness, how deeply I miss all of you with the affection of Christ Jesus.*
> **PHILIPPIANS 1:3-8**

LEADING THROUGH HARD THINGS

Paul took the initiative to lead in a very difficult and divided culture. Philippi was a complicated mess, struggling through a complex history. There was prejudice and political strife. As a result of the Battle of Actium (31 BC), the city of Philippi was re-founded as a Roman colony. This meant that the conquering Roman soldiers and their families remade the city into a Roman colony. The victorious Romans enjoyed all the fruits of being a citizen in the newly colonized city, while the indigenous people were discriminated against.

It was a seemingly impossible scenario. To make matters worse, Paul couldn't be there in person. He was imprisoned and had to help them from hundreds of miles away, communicating by letter. Paul displayed an unmistakable leadership lesson: *leaders take the initiative to do hard things*.

When have you seen someone lead through difficult circumstances?

AN ATTITUDE OF GRATITUDE

Paul also demonstrated that an attitude of gratitude is one of the most effective ways to serve and earn the right to have difficult conversations (which he did later on in chapter 1). It is clear within the first few verses of Philippians that Paul had a personal love for the church in Philippi. In Philippians 1:3-8, he demonstrated for us how to build up the believers through gratitude:

➤ Paul reminded them of their shared history: Shared memories enable the leader to speak into the culture. "I give thanks to my God for every remembrance of you" (Phil. 1:3).

➤ Paul genuinely liked the people in the church at Philippi: Sincerely caring for people is essential to influencing as a disciple. "Always praying with joy for all of you in my every prayer" (Phil 1:4).

➤ Paul valued collaborating with them: Healthy leaders understand the value and benefits of we versus me. "Because of your partnership in the gospel from the first day until now" (Phil 1:5).

➤ Paul believed the best about all the Philippian believers and sought to build them up: Accentuating the positive is a honoring approach to leadership. "I am sure of this, that he who started a good work in you will carry it on to completion until the day of Christ Jesus" (Phil 1:6).

➤ Paul was transparent about the genuine emotions he had for them: Expressing warm and authentic words is never wasted energy. "I have you in my heart, and you are all partners with me in grace, both in my imprisonment and in the defense and confirmation of the gospel. For God is my witness, how deeply I miss all of you with the affection of Christ Jesus" (Phil 1:7-8).

Discussion Questions

How has God taken the initiative with humanity?

How does God, in His goodness, continue to take the initiative with us?

Take a few moments to discuss how Paul took the initiative with the Philippians.

Paul uses words of gratitude to begin his letter. Why is the attitude of gratitude important to leadership?

How can we practice taking the initiative? How can we practice gratitude?

Take a sheet of paper and write out 3-4 sentences to a person or group of people you are grateful for. Use the five ideas that Paul demonstrated in Philippians 1:3-8 (see page 10).

DAY 1
FOUR WAYS TO STAY FOREVER GRATEFUL

Remember God is at Work in Our Sufferings

We have seen the amazing, brave, and faithful initiative Paul took when he planted the church at Philippi, the first church on the continent of Europe. Yet the circumstances he found himself in as he wrote his letter were less than ideal. He had to express his gratitude all while being chained away in a dark prison. If ever there was an individual whose circumstances could have given him reason not to be grateful, it would have been Paul. Here is a shortlist of some of what he endured:

➤ There were multiple attempts and plots on his life (Acts 9:23-29; 20:3; 21:30; 23:10,12; 25:3).

➤ He was stoned and left for dead (Acts 14:19).

➤ He endured satanic attacks and pressure (1 Thess. 2:18).

➤ He was beaten and jailed in Philippi (Acts 16:19-24).

➤ He suffered name-calling and ridicule (Acts 17:16-18; 26:24).

➤ He was falsely accused (Acts 21:21,28; 24:5-9).

➤ On five occasions, he was given thirty-nine lashes by the Jews (2 Cor. 11:24).

➤ He was beaten with rods three times by the Romans (2 Cor. 11:25).

➤ He survived numerous violent storms at sea (2 Cor. 11:25; Acts 27:14-20).

➤ He was bitten by a poisonous snake (Acts 28:3-4).

➤ He was forsaken by friends and co-laborers (2 Tim. 4:10,16).

If I were Paul, the minute a poisonous snake bit me, I would've been out of there. But Paul endured unimaginable pressure and pain. Instead he wrote:

> *We are afflicted in every way but not crushed; we are perplexed but not in despair; we are persecuted but not abandoned; we are struck down but not destroyed.... Indeed everything is for your benefit so that, as grace extends through more and more people, it may cause thanksgiving to increase to the glory of God*
> **2 CORINTHIANS 4:8-9,15**

Paul's perspective can leave one speechless. All the assassination attempts, all the imprisonments, all the backstabbing, and deception, battling mother nature at sea and on land, all of it was to further the gospel. He was grateful for what he had endured so that people could experience Jesus, which is cause for thanksgiving.

More lives changed = More grateful people = Paul becoming more and more grateful. What a perspective!

God was present in the sufferings, and He was redeeming the pain so others could experience peace. I'm so glad we get a backstage pass to Paul's scars. Each scar is just a different memory of God using physical hurt to bring about someone's spiritual healing. Knowing God is at work on the good days and the ones when we suffer for His name's sake, and that He allows us to be a part of the story He is telling—that's a reason for gratitude.

How have you seen God work in your own seasons of suffering?

> *Close your time today with a season of grateful prayer. Even if you can't see how God is using your suffering, pray knowing that He can and will.*

DAY 2
FOUR WAYS TO STAY FOREVER GRATEFUL

Remember God's Presence in Our Provision

He who started a good work in you will carry it on to completion until the day of Christ Jesus.
PHILIPPIANS 1:6

Paul wanted the Philippian believers to know that it is Jesus—and Jesus alone—who could complete the good work that had begun in them. God was at work and would always be at work in them. If this is true, God's enduring presence in us is God's unfailing provision for us. Furthermore, if God is ever-present, then there is always a reason to be grateful.

How have you experienced God's presence in your life to this point?

If God is always with us, then one of the greatest exercises a human can ever do is to practice the presence of God.[3] Practicing the presence of God is an idea that has been long discussed. People have written books, taught seminars, and held retreats all aimed at wrestling with this idea. How do we practice the presence of God? In short, we practice the presence of God when we take the necessary steps to stay aware of God's presence in our lives. Some practices include morning and evening prayers, taking time each day to meditate on something in Scripture, and having plans that tear down any barriers that keep us from focusing on God. For example: when I start to feel like complaining today, I will use that as an opportunity for praise or prayer.

What is another way you can flip a barrier to God's presence into an opportunity to experience Him today?

The more we pursue experiencing God's presence, the more grateful we will become. Paul demonstrated this in Colossians 2:6-7: "So then, just as you have received Christ Jesus as Lord, continue to walk in him … overflowing with gratitude." Living with Jesus can only make us grateful.

Take some time to think about and journal more steps you can take to be continually aware of God's presence and grace in your life. It may be helpful to recognize barriers that distract from experiencing God's presence. Then identify ways to overcome those barriers. Another habit I practice is to set an alarm for what I know will be the busiest part of my day. When it goes off, I pause to pray and spend a few moments being grateful for Jesus. Even if I'm in the middle of a very important meeting, no one seems to mind. They usually see it as an invitation to pray themselves. And before it is all over, we all pray together. This little practice helps focus the affections of my heart, redeem the moments at hand, and reminds me that God's presence is God's provision during a time of the day when God might be far from my thoughts.

What are three steps you can take to be more aware of God's presence?

1.

2.

3.

What are two barriers to being aware of God's presence in your life?

Identify one way you can be more grateful today for Jesus.

Close your time today in prayer using some of the strategies you just developed to experience God's presence.

DAY 3
FOUR WAYS TO STAY FOREVER GRATEFUL

Remember God Wants Us to Know and Be Known

A third way to cultivate a lifestyle of gratitude is through authentic relationships. The words of Paul in Philippians 1:7 are beautiful, "I have you in my heart, and you are all partners with me in grace." Paul's heart was emotionally bound to the people of the church at Philippi. He knew them, and they knew him. The Christ-followers in Philippi were aware of Paul's needs and had continually sent him gifts for his work (4:15-18). God had shown His kindness to Paul through the people of faith in Philippi.

Who has been a blessing to you?

God often uses others to demonstrate His love towards us. That is why it is crucial to have healthy relationships. We all need individuals in our lives who act like doctors and patients of each other's souls—having a genuine care for each other. One kind of relationship that is vital is healthy friendships. Friendships for leaders are often a challenging task. Ungodly thoughts such as, *does this person enhance my brand* and *I don't want to trust anyone*, if left unchecked, can go through our heads.

What is another barrier to authentic relationships in your life?

But if you are going to be a disciple who takes their influence seriously, healthy and authentic friendships are indispensable.

Four characteristics should describe your friendships:

1. Friends prioritize presence over productivity. This means being present for each other is more important than what we can get from each other.
2. Friends don't have to qualify to receive quality. This means friends don't have to achieve a standard of perfection to receive love and compassion.
3. Friends seek to understand before being understood. This means friends first carefully listen to each other and then offer thoughtful advice.
4. Friends are quick to set aside themselves in order to sacrifice. This means friends have the needs of others in their hearts.

One of the greatest movies ever to grace the silver screen is the classic 1946 Christmas film, *It's a Wonderful Life*. The story chronicles the struggles and frustrations of George Baily. George had big dreams of traveling the world to build tall buildings in important places. Yet, at every turn, he was thwarted by obstacles and bad luck. In the depth of his frustration and a suicide attempt, an angel named Clarence was sent to save him. George Baily had grown to believe it would have been better if he had never been born. By the end of the movie, he realizes that the love of his family, friends, and the town he had dedicated himself to offered him immeasurable riches. As the movie comes to a close, Clarence the angel leaves George a copy of a book with the inscription: "Dear George: Remember no man is a failure who has friends. Thanks for the wings! Love, Clarence."[4]

Friendship is a gift from God that allows us to know others and be known. God did not design us to live on our own. He designed us for relationships. Relationships cultivate gratefulness in our hearts.

What is a relationship that needs some attention in your life?

Close your time today in prayer reviewing the four characteristics of friendship. Ask God to cultivate these attitudes and habits in your friendships.

DAY 4
FOUR WAYS TO STAY FOREVER GRATEFUL

Remember God is the Giver of Good Gifts

James, the brother of Jesus, wrote, "Every good and perfect gift is from above, coming down from the Father of lights, who does not change like shifting shadows" (James 1:17). Paul had experienced good gifts from the Philippians, but the trustworthy source of those gifts was God the Father.

What is a gift you have received from someone else, but you know came straight from the heart of God the Father?

According to James, there are two ways we can know that a gift is from God. First, it's "good," meaning that there is nothing sinful about the gift. Second, the gift is "perfect," which is a word that expands upon good, emphasizing the moral quality of the gift.[5]

It is difficult for some of us to understand that God actually wants to bless His sons and daughters. A very insightful pastor wrote:

> One of the enemy's tricks is to convince us that our Father is holding out on us, that He does not really love us and care for us. When Satan approached Eve, he suggested that if God really loved her, He would permit her to eat the forbidden tree.[6]

What is one lie that Satan tries to convince you of about God?

Now let's be honest about something: God can and will bless people in different ways. God has a plan and a mission; a story that He is telling and He's the only one who knows how everything works together. Our responsibility is to be grateful and use the gifts He gives us honorably.

What is one way God has blessed someone differently from how He has blessed you?

Some people have different Spiritual gifts than others (Rom. 12:3-8). There are also different talents, looks, and abilities people have. One person might be incredibly athletic, another musical, and still another a mathlete. The point is, don't compare your gifts, talents, looks, or abilities to someone else, but spend your time recognizing the Giver of the gift and being grateful.

List three gifts, talents, or abilities God has given you.

1.

2.

3.

List a way you can use each gift, talent, or ability to honor the Giver of every good and perfect gift.

I know it sounds old-fashioned, but sit down and just begin writing out all the ways God has blessed you. If you're stumped on how to begin, start with the fact that the sun came up this morning. Recognizing the goodness of God in His blessings to us is another incredible way to nurture a spirit of gratitude.

Take some time to write out your prayer of gratitude today.

SESSION 2

THE EXCELLENT, BOLD, OPTIMISTIC LEADER

VIDEO GUIDE

INTERVIEW: Chaplain Barry Black

SCRIPTURE:

And I pray this: that your love will keep on growing in knowledge and every kind of discernment, so that you may approve the things that are superior and may be pure and blameless in the day of Christ, filled with the fruit of righteousness that comes through Jesus Christ to the glory and praise of God.
PHILIPPIANS 1:9-11

NOTES:

INTERESTING QUOTE:

KEY POINTS:

Evangeline

I once met a woman who was a volunteer at an institution for people who were mentally ill. Let's call her Evangeline. She introduced me to her world for the overlooked in our society. She embodied so many leadership qualities and characteristics though she never held a fancy title.

As we walked down the hall, I asked questions about her work and patients. She quickly and kindly rebuked me, "These are not my patients, they are my friends." I was introduced to Evangeline's friends one by one. Each room presented a human being with different challenges that required a unique, loving, and creative solution. Each room had been transformed into a world saturated with love and creativity. Here are a few examples of what I witnessed:

A woman believed the hospital clothes were hurting her skin, so Evangeline had filled a closet with clothes made from "special" fabric that would protect her.

An elderly man loved Mr. Pibb, believing Dr. Pepper was the enemy. His refrigerator was stocked with, you guessed it, Mr. Pibb.

Another man self-harmed for years until Evangeline discovered his love for country music legend Kenny Rogers. Now the soothing sounds of the bearded wonder help create a calm world where the man can control his impulses to hurt himself.

A woman who had been institutionalized for most of her life and had not spoken for years, found a friend in Evangeline. This woman had been homeless and had lost a baby early in her life. On the day I met her, she held a baby doll, given to her by Evangeline, and was capable of communicating.

Evangeline lived her life among the outcasts and overlooked of this world. Believing deeply in the person and work of Jesus led her to unashamedly befriend and care for people. In turn, such boldness based in love enabled her to believe and envision the best for those who had experienced the worst of a broken world. Evangeline created worlds in concrete rooms. She helped redeem the realities of those who had been beaten down by a broken world, and in the process, she pointed people to the Redeemer. She did all this because leadership begins at the feet of Jesus.

EXCELLENCE, BOLDNESS, AND OPTIMISM

Evangeline's approach to leadership is special, but it isn't new. In fact, it is the very approach Paul demonstrated for us in Philippians 1. Philippi experienced the same polarization that has come to characterize our society. As disciples who care about our influence and desire to use it for the glory of Christ, we must ask this question: how do we lead as followers of Jesus in a divided culture?

The book of Philippians provides instructions to help us discover the answer.

1. Excellence is continuing to love what is best.

Philippians 1:9-11 can be called "the prayer that changed a city."

> *And I pray this: that your love will keep on growing in knowledge and every kind of discernment, so that you may approve the things that are superior and may be pure and blameless in the day of Christ, filled with the fruit of righteousness that comes through Jesus Christ to the glory and praise of God.*
> **PHILIPPIANS 1:9-11**

Paul's prayer shows the progression of a growing love:

1. A growing love leads us to know and live truth, while increasing in discernment: "That your love will keep on growing in knowledge and every kind of discernment" (Phil. 1:9).
2. Growing in knowledge and discernment creates an appetite for excellence: "So that you may approve the things that are superior" (Phil. 1:10a).
3. An appetite for excellence enables us to live an authentic life: "And may be pure and blameless in the day of Christ" (Phil. 1:10b).
4. An authentic life increasingly demonstrates a fruitfulness that reveals a growing love: "Filled with the fruit of righteousness that comes through Jesus Christ to the glory and praise of God" (Phil. 1:11).

A leader will never rise higher than the depth of love they possess. Leadership begins with a growing love, and the result in our lives will be the ability to know what really matters to God and to live accordingly.

How have you seen love bridge a divide in a group of people?

2. Boldness is confidently confirming what is best.

A growing love leads to an unashamed and bold desire to maximize one's influence for the name of Jesus, regardless of circumstance.

> *Now I want you to know, brothers and sisters, that what has happened to me has actually advanced the gospel, so that it has become known throughout the whole imperial guard, and to everyone else, that my imprisonment is because I am in Christ. Most of the brothers have gained confidence in the Lord from my imprisonment and dare even more to speak the word fearlessly.*
>
> **PHILIPPIANS 1:12-14**

Paul's growing love led to him being imprisoned. However, his imprisonment led to a bold, contagious spread of the gospel that spilled into the imperial guard and the church in Rome. Boldness is an outward expression of a deeply held belief, fueled by a growing love. Boldness doesn't mean that one becomes arrogant or a bully for the gospel. We can be bold while not abandoning God's love or our unique personality and creativity.

What Paul wanted, not only for the Philippians but for all who would read his message, could be summarized as a growing love that positions us to have a divine perspective in even the most difficult of circumstances. A divine perspective affords us the boldness to confidently confirm what is best.

When have you been bold as a result of your growing love for Christ?

3. Optimism is believing and hoping for the best.

Great leaders don't just tell you what to do, they demonstrate it. In Philippians 1:21, Paul demonstrated the depth of his optimistic outlook, writing, "For me, to live is Christ and to die is gain." My favorite way of defining optimism is an undeterred belief and hope that the best is always yet to come. We can always be optimistic because with Jesus anything is possible!

Paul wanted the Philippians to embrace this optimism so that the seemingly impossible divide in their culture could be bridged. That is why he wrote:

Just one thing: As citizens of heaven, live your life worthy of the gospel of Christ. Then, whether I come and see you or am absent, I will hear about you that you are standing firm in one spirit, in one accord, contending together for the faith of the gospel.

PHILIPPIANS 1:27

After demonstrating optimism concerning his own life, he hoped for "just one thing," that they would awaken to the reality that a new citizenship has been granted. The culture was divided over citizenship, the haves and the have nots, but Paul was saying that they have both been granted a new citizenship, one that is infinitely superior to anything that human armies could accomplish. It is not that the past was no longer relevant, past injustice should never be swept under the rug. Paul was explaining to them that they were no longer strangers, but family—sons and daughters of God—no longer separate, but together!

Discussion Questions

How can Paul's threefold excellence strategy (growing love, boldness, and optimism) help bridge divides that we see in our world today?

How does having a growing love impact those around us? What happens when our love ceases to grow or begins to struggle to grow?

How do we know the line between boldness and being overbearing? How can we strive for boldness while still maintaining a firm grasp on God's love?

How can we remain optimistic, but not oblivious to the realities of our world?

DAY 1
FOUR REASONS TO BE OPTIMISTIC

Our Identity is "Citizen of Heaven"

Followers of Jesus should be the most optimistic people in any culture. Since we hold tightly to a hope that cannot fail, we are always positioned to hope and believe (Rom. 5:5). This week we will focus on four reasons for optimism. As a reminder, we aren't talking about optimism based on subjective sentiment and wishful thinking devoid of the reality of objective truth. In other words, we aren't the meme of the dog sitting in the cafe as it burns down around him saying, "This is fine." No, ours is an optimism rooted in the person and work of Jesus. Our conversion to Christianity enables us to have a divine perspective on the brokenness of a world shattered by sin.

What's the difference between being optimistic and oblivious?

Let's start at the beginning of our life in Christ. When Jesus made us new creations, our identity was transformed from the inside out. We are now "citizens of heaven" and are to live our lives "worthy of the gospel of Christ" (Phil. 1:27). When God redeemed us through the finished work of His Son, Jesus, we got a new address: heaven. In other words, Jesus moved into the neighborhood of humanity, so humanity could one day move into His neighborhood in heaven. Because of our new address, we strive to live our lives worthy of the gospel. Simply put, we do this by filtering everything about this life on earth through our heavenly citizenship. It is a beautiful thing to live with your head in the clouds and feet firmly planted on the ground. Being a citizen of heaven determines the way we live, laugh, and love.

When have you made the difficult choice to filter something out of your life because you are now a citizen of heaven?

So, what does this have to do with optimism? *Everything.* If life is a journey towards our heavenly address, then the best is always yet to come. God has made it possible for us to live every day with glorious anticipation. And it is practically impossible to be pessimistic while being captivated by the beauty of what God has accomplished and the destination of the journey. Our optimism is rooted in our salvation.

Create a pro and con list for being optimistic over pessimistic.

PRO	CON

The world needs optimists whose perspective is motivated by Jesus. Individuals who rise above the noise of cancel culture, throwing shade, and using people's worst moments as a form of entertainment. God calls us to be influencers who believe and hope for what is best, because our very identity attests to a better way. He wants us to be optimists that envision a way forward because the journey towards heaven doesn't take a U-turn.

> Today let's ask God for the perspective needed to convey the hope within us. Pray that God gives you the motivation, willingness, and endurance to be an everyday optimist.

DAY 2
FOUR REASONS TO BE OPTIMISTIC

God Doesn't Play the Odds

One of my favorite things to witness is when God shows off and defies human logic. Scripture is filled with examples of God bewildering all who would observe. It is astonishing to think that God can use who He wants, when He wants, to accomplish what He wants. He can even use people without any prior experience! For example:

- Noah had never seen a flood, much less an ocean (Gen. 7:6-9).
- Sarah had never been pregnant (Gen. 17:17-22).
- Joshua had never led a nation (Joshua 1:1-9).
- David had never killed a giant (1 Sam. 17).
- Josiah had never been king (2 Kings 22:1-2).
- Nehemiah had never built a wall (Neh. 2).
- Esther had never been queen (Esther 2:15-18).
- Isaiah had never seen the Lord (Isa. 6:1-8).
- Mary and Joseph had never been parents (Luke 2:1-7).
- Paul had never preached the gospel (Acts 9:19-25).

Which of these long shot stories resonates most with your heart?

How God used the leadership of the apostle Paul in the city of Philippi is just another example in a long history of examples of "the odds don't concern God." Consider this:

Paul spent nearly six years of his adult life incarcerated with two of his prison terms being served in Rome. He was being guarded by the most powerful, elite military unit in the world. He was under the authority of a tyrannical psychopath emperor who was probably still a teenager and believed himself to be a deity. Hence, Nero felt threatened by and hated Christians. And Paul was trying to help a church plant in a city over four thousand miles away overcome division and prejudice that dated back nearly one hundred years.

Hmmm, I think Paul definitely had the odds stacked against him in this scenario. Vegas wouldn't have even called the situation a long shot—impossible is a more appropriate description. Yet, this is how Paul described what God was doing with his circumstances:

> *Now I want you to know, brothers and sisters, that what has happened to me has actually advanced the gospel, so that it has become known throughout the whole imperial guard, and to everyone else, that my imprisonment is because I am in Christ.*
> **PHILIPPIANS 1:12-13**

If God doesn't played the odds, then neither should we. We simply need to be able to answer the questions: Can I trust God when the odds seem insurmountable? Do I believe that God can redeem any situation for His purposes? Is my perspective that God can make a way when there is no way? He has a long history of doing so.

> *Pray about a long shot situation in your life. Ask God to help you be optimistic about the situation and believe with all your heart that He has it totally under control. Pray that regardless of the outcome, He would be glorified and your trust in Him would only grow deeper.*

DAY 3
FOUR REASONS TO BE OPTIMISTIC

Even Our Scars Can Tell the Story of God's Goodness

There is an optimism that is seldom seen or experienced. But those rare souls who express this divine perspective are like a great piece of art. The longer one ponders its beauty, the more depth of meaning and significance is discovered. I am speaking of suffering, and more specifically the scars incurred from life. Paul wrote of it this way:

> *For it has been granted to you on Christ's behalf not only to believe in him, but also to suffer for him, since you are engaged in the same struggle that you saw I had and now hear that I have.*
> **PHILIPPIANS 1:29-30**

Think about this. In one of the most upbeat letters from one of the greatest leaders the world has ever known, he basically said: "hey guys, hang on, the story doesn't just end with the gift of salvation, there's something else!" And that something else is suffering. Eugene Peterson interpreted it this way: "There's far more to this life than trusting in Christ. There's also suffering for him. And the suffering is as much a gift as the trusting" (Phil. 1:29-30, MSG). Suffering is a gift? My first thought is, *does this gift come with a receipt?*

How could suffering ever be considered a gift?

There is no receipt because God graces us with suffering so that we can know the sufficiency of Christ and the power of His resurrection (see Phil. 3:10). It allows us to identify with Christ and know that we are never alone in our sufferings. Through our sufferings we must refuse to remain silent or passive. They bear witness to the grace of Jesus in our lives and our response to it. Our response is our opportunity to influence. While we shouldn't seek out suffering, we should not retreat from it either. We view it with the divine perspective—optimism—as a gift to be used for the glory of God and the advancement of the gospel. When God allows us to suffer for His name's sake, He is trusting us to use our influence for what matters most.

How does our suffering for His name give us an opportunity to advance the gospel and be a person of influence?

The longer we live the more scars we accumulate. Don't hide them; don't waste them. Those scars accumulated "on Christ's behalf" (1:29) all tell a story of how God loved us enough to trust us. Allow your scars to be beautiful reminders that Jesus is always close, that we can know his sufficiency, and that our influence matters. And when you tell the story of your scars, do so in a way that people are astonished by your perspective on past pain. Let your scars be the rare works of art that cause people to stop and wonder, and the longer they ponder the more significance and meaning they discover. Before long the amazement of it all leaves them with one conclusion—the amazing grace of Jesus.

List one or more times you've suffered in the past and how God has used it to advance His kingdom:

> *Today, pray that you would be the rare soul with a divine perspective and an optimism that can't be shaken. Pray that you would be a person who will drawn close to Jesus in the tough times and remain undeterred in your hope in all the days to come.*

DAY 4
FOUR REASONS TO BE OPTIMISTIC

Together We Can Accomplish Great Things

Paul wanted the Christians in Philippi to discover the beauty of togetherness. It seems that we live in a time that makes unity, oneness, or togetherness the ultimate goal. Let's understand this clearly: our togetherness isn't the goal, rather it is the result of living our lives worthy of the gospel. It is through embracing our heavenly citizenship that harmony and togetherness become the reality desired by so many. Paul wanted the Philippian Christians to experience this: "whether I come and see you or am absent, I will hear about you that you are standing firm in one spirit, in one accord, contending together for the faith of the gospel" (1:27).

Consider where—together—we once were.

➤ Together, we listened to the wrong voice and ate the fruit.
➤ Together, we were lost and alone in the wilderness.
➤ Together, we grew comfortable with the walls being torn down and living in the rubble or our rebellion.
➤ Together, we were once half dead on the side of the road desperate for one more breath.
➤ Together, we were begging at the city gates hoping for kindness.
➤ Together, we were once lost, scared, hopeless, prideful, and shame-filled.

When was a time, together with others, you found yourself going down the wrong path?

Then Jesus moved into the neighborhood and gave us a new identity. *Now …*

- Together, we see God's beauty and grace His creation.
- Together, we have been made alive to run and live redeemed.
- Together, we never have to beg again because we are children of the King.
- Together, we are found, hope-filled, humble, and free.

When was a time, together with others, you celebrated what you share together in Christ?

There is beauty in our togetherness, but also incredible influence to be discovered. When we contend together for the faith, Christ is glorified, our togetherness grows, and the desired will of God is pursued. There is a collective influence, a bigger story being told when Christians have the right attitude and a focused mindset. Together, we can change the world according to the desires of God's heart.

- Only together can we be witnesses for Jesus to the ends of the earth.
- Only together can we do the hard work of justice.
- Only together can we care for the marginalized and overlooked in our culture.
- Only together can we build strong churches that make disciples who also make disciples.
- Only together can we can do good works that lead people to give glory to our Father in heaven.

> *Together, all of this is possible and more. The beauty and power of togetherness should give birth to optimism that thinks critically and creatively. Make your own "together" list, share it with other citizens of heaven, and spend some time imagining and praying about how it could be when we work together.*

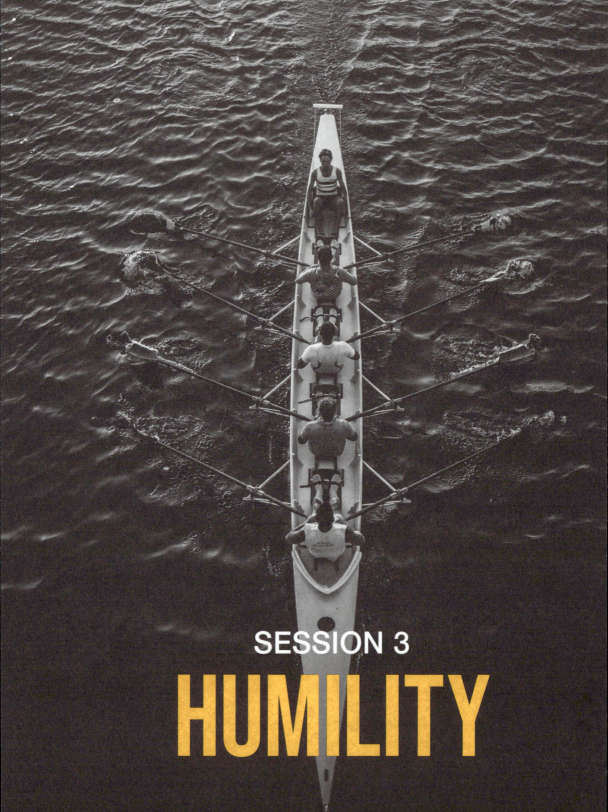

VIDEO GUIDE

INTERVIEW: Colonel Kim Poole

SCRIPTURE:

Do nothing out of selfish ambition or conceit, but in humility consider others as more important than yourselves. Everyone should look not to his own interests, but rather to the interests of others.
PHILIPPIANS 2:3-4

NOTES:

INTERESTING QUOTE:

KEY POINTS:

The Story Less Told

Every leader has a coming-of-age chapter in their story. Truth be known, there are only two options for this chapter. The first option can be referred to as "fake-it-till-you-make-it." It looks really good on the surface—and social media. It can lead to a lot of attention and praise, but is an exhausting approach to life and leadership. It's very self focused. The problem with "fake-it-till-you-make-it" is that, in the end, we just become professional fakers. It leaves the leader feeling empty, despite the resume of successes or the number of views and followers.

The second option is fulfilling in a way that cannot be fully captured on a social media platform or even a real-life-turned-docu-drama series that premiers on your favorite streaming service. It's fulfilling because it focuses on the needs and service of others. It satisfies something fundamental for the disciple: when we follow Jesus, it will lead us to serve others.

It is a fascinating paradox: the more a leader tries to succeed by elevating himself, the unhealthier and emptier that individual becomes. Yet, the more a leader pours out in service to others, the more that individual experiences health and gratifying purpose.

As emerging leaders at the beginning of your story, two possible roads are before you to choose. One road is crowded and scarred up by the clutter of competing brands and self-centered narratives. The other is increasingly less crowded and lies before you with a sacred simplicity. The first follows a vision determined by self, about self, and for self; the second follows a renegade Rabbi who literally was the incarnation of God's hope for humanity.

I pray you choose to follow the Rabbi's road and approach to influence. While prominence and power cannot be promised down that road, you will be following the Redeemer who was pierced because of the rebellion of the world (see Isaiah 53:5).

For those who choose the story less told, let's discover how to be a leader who walks with a spirit of humility.

HUMILITY DEFINED: CONSIDER OTHERS

Remember that Paul was writing into a polarized culture in Philippi. Another way of defining the phrase *polarized culture* is "a place where differing viewpoints have led individuals to see the other as the opposition." Paul modeled and wrote about a beautiful truth that deconstructed entitlement, pride, self-righteousness, and anything that resulted from living in a divided culture: the gospel requires us to always consider others.

> *Do nothing out of selfish ambition or conceit, but in humility, consider others as more important than yourselves. Everyone should look not to his own interests, but rather to the interests of others.*
> **PHILIPPIANS 2:3-4**

Let's break these verses down so we can see this definition of humility emerge more clearly:

➤ Considering others begins with rejecting pride: "Do nothing out of selfish ambition or conceit" (Phil 2:3a).

➤ Considering others is proven by valuing other people as "more important": "In humility, consider others more important than yourself" (Phil 2:3b).

➤ Considering others is a mentality that doesn't seek to exalt self: "Everyone should look not to his own interests, but rather to the interests of others" (Phil. 2:4).

The Greek word translated as "humility" was also used to describe the Nile River during the dry season when it runs low.[1] The picture of the Nile being full versus running low provides for us an incredible image to further inform our understanding of humility. When a disciple of Jesus who seeks to influence others is full of selfish ambition, pride, and a story too often told, that leader becomes ineffective.

When have you seen a leader become too full of selfish ambition and pride and become ineffective?

Go back to Philippians 2:1-2 to see the motivations for humility on full display in the blessings of the Christian community:

PHILIPPIANS

> *If, then, there is any encouragement in Christ, if any consolation of love, if any fellowship with the Spirit, if any affection and mercy, make my joy complete by thinking the same way, having the same love, united in spirit, intent on one purpose.*
> **PHILIPPIANS 2:1-2**

Again, let's break down the verses to see the reality more clearly:

➤ Together we are all committed to Jesus and have a shared source for our encouragement: "If, then, there is any encouragement in Christ" (Phil. 2:1a).

➤ Together we're comforted by the love of Jesus: "If any consolation of love" (Phil. 2:1b).

➤ Together we are part of a community because the same Holy Spirit is working in all of us: "If any fellowship with the Spirit" (Phil. 2:1c).

➤ Together we have experienced the compassion of Jesus: "If any affection and mercy" (Phil. 2:1d).

➤ Together we can be like-minded in love and in purpose: "Make my joy complete by thinking the same way, having the same love, united in spirit, intent on one purpose" (Phil 2:2).

How does community help build humility as followers of Christ?

The example of Jesus leads us to adopt the attitude of Jesus.

> *Adopt the same attitude as that of Christ Jesus, who, existing in the form of God, did not consider equality with God as something to be exploited. Instead he emptied himself by assuming the form of a servant, taking on the likeness of humanity. And when he had come as a man, he humbled himself by becoming obedient to the point of death—even to death on a cross.*
> **PHILIPPIANS 2:5-8**

The word *adopt* is powerful and immediately stirs up the image of a family bringing a child who was not born to them into their home. Just like a child is chosen when they are adopted, we must choose to have the attitude of Jesus. In choosing "the same attitude as that of Christ Jesus" (2:5), we are deciding to internally think in a way that doesn't come naturally. But because Jesus is transforming us from the inside out, we can choose to follow His example. This is when things start to get really exciting, because this is when our lives begin to align with the heart of Jesus.

It is not an overstatement to say that humility is the most important characteristic of a disciple who wants to influence like Jesus. After all, "God resists the proud but gives grace to the humble" (James 4:6). This is why the example of Jesus is so important. His life and sacrifice modeled for us that humility is an attitude absent of ego and self-interest, while being fixated on radical obedience to God and doing what is good for others.

Practicing an others-first mentality conditions our hearts and minds to walk with a spirit of humility. Therefore, let's practice considering others.

Discussion Questions

Who is an individual in your life that has chosen the story less told by making a practice of considering others in their leadership journey?

How can you prioritize the interests of others as you seek to be an influencer for God's kingdom?

List some examples from the life of Jesus where He emptied Himself and served others. What does someone having the same attitude as Jesus look like? How can you demonstrate this same humility in your life?

DAY 1
FOUR ADOPTABLE WAYS JESUS WAS HUMBLE

Generosity: Jesus Valued Proximity Over Privilege

Adopt the same attitude as that of Christ Jesus, who, existing in the form of God, did not consider equality with God as something to be exploited. Instead, he emptied himself by assuming the form of a servant, taking on the likeness of humanity.
PHILIPPIANS 2:5-7

Jesus's "taking on the likeness of humanity" is the single most generous act in the history of the universe. The generosity of God is that Jesus became one of us. By becoming one of us, He put Himself in proximity to all of us. In *The Message*, Eugene Peterson described God's generosity this way: "The Word became flesh and blood, and moved into the neighborhood" (John 1:14, MSG).

God's generosity makes life, joy, and hope possible. We are invited to adopt His attitude—to choose to be generous like Jesus. The world is filled with so-called leaders who want to position and posture their way to influence. It's a hollow strategy that seems to dissolve like cotton candy in water. Generosity, on the other hand, is an approach to leadership that will bear lasting fruit.

The type of generosity that Jesus demonstrated guides us to have proximity, or closeness, to those we influence. It's impossible to emulate Jesus's model for leadership without having a presence and intentionality about building relationships among those we seek to influence. To put it simply: you can't be an effective leader from a distance.

I realize that this may seem elementary and simplistic, but we live in a world of social media influence. We hope for something to go viral that gives us the platform to be "influencers." Because of the ever-expanding digital footprint we are all creating, it's worth noting that the most important and consequential leader in history focused on building positive and lasting relationships with only a small group of people. That small group of people went and changed the world.

Consider someone you know who is an impactful leader and is also relational. List the qualities or characteristics that make him or her so effective at being relational. Is he or she a good listener? Thoughtful? Helpful?

List some of the qualities that make Jesus such a relational leader.

Create a list of qualities or characteristics that you would like to adopt into your own life and leadership.

> *Pray that you would become or continue to walk with a spirit of humility and generosity. Talk to God about your list and commit to pursuing each quality or characteristic.*

DAY 2
FOUR ADOPTABLE WAYS JESUS WAS HUMBLE

Servant: Jesus Chose Self-Denial Over Self-Interest

Adopt the same attitude as that of Christ Jesus, who, existing in the form of God, did not consider equality with God as something to be exploited. Instead he emptied himself by assuming the form of a servant, taking on the likeness of humanity.

PHILIPPIANS 2:5-7

The entire mission of Jesus is characterized by self-denial. The generosity of God can be summed up in one word: proximity. Once Jesus drew near to us, His actions can be summarized with another word: servant. The selflessness of Jesus characterized the ministry and leadership of Jesus. On one occasion, Jesus said, "the Son of Man did not come to be served, but to serve, and to give his life as a ransom for many" (Matt. 20:28). In the upper room shortly before He was arrested, Jesus washed each of the disciple's feet. This was done out of humility, as an act of service, and to model how they were to treat one another. The leadership of Jesus teaches us to draw near to others so that we might serve them.

List three additional ways Jesus served others during His time on earth.

It is a rare thing to discover a leader who is willing to put others' needs and welfare above themselves. The world is full of people shouting to be heard, clamoring to be seen, and longing to be admired. There seems to be a shortage of people who are willing to care for others beyond the camera's reach and minister to needs when no one is looking. From the upper room, Jesus taught us that a life spent washing feet is never wasted.

List three ways you can "wash the feet" of others today.

If Jesus, the Savior of the world, "assumed the form of a servant," then how can aspiring leaders today expect anything different for their lives? Assuming the form of a servant is only way that we can even begin to follow the example of Jesus's leadership.

Finally, it should be noted that following this example often leads us to unexpected places and discovering stories that need to be heard. Stories of pain, loneliness, and hopelessness are often among the forgotten or overlooked.

> *Pray that by assuming the posture of service, we might enter into being a servant among the broken and have their stories transformed into examples of hope, community, and purpose.*

DAY 3
FOUR ADOPTABLE WAYS JESUS WAS HUMBLE

Sacrifice: He Demonstrated Obedience to the Purpose Over Self-Preservation

And when he had come as a man, he humbled himself by becoming obedient to the point of death—even to death on a cross.
PHILIPPIANS 2:7-8

God's generosity means that Jesus moved into the neighborhood of humanity so that He could serve humanity. Yet, the most remarkable thing Jesus did was to be obedient to God's ultimate plan for redeeming us by sacrificing His life. In the same sentence that Paul wrote, "when he had come as a man," he also wrote, "by becoming obedient to the point of death—even to death on a cross." Paul wanted us to see that Jesus was both small enough and big enough. He was both the child who was born to us and the King of kings and Lord of lords. As one of my college professors used to say, "Jesus is the only 200 percent being ever to exist. One hundred percent man and one hundred percent God."

Think about it. Jesus was:

➤ Small enough to be born into the world,
    big enough to have spoken everything into existence (Col. 1:16).

➤ Small enough to be born in Bethlehem, the "City of Bread,"
    big enough to be the "Bread of Life" (John 6:35).

➤ Small enough to be born into a young family,
    big enough to welcome all who would come into His family (Matt. 11:28).

- ➤ Small enough for an old woman after a lifetime of waiting (Luke 2:36-38),
  big enough for all who are waiting.

- ➤ Small enough to wash feet,
  big enough to have His own feet nailed to a cross (Col. 2:14).

- ➤ Small enough, for our sake, to become poor,
  big enough that through His poverty, we might become rich (2 Cor. 8:9).

- ➤ Small enough to live a life free from the captivity of sin,
  big enough to bear all the sins of the world and set His people free (Isa. 53:4).

- ➤ Small enough to need swaddling cloths,
  big enough to one day leave His burial cloths behind (John 20:7).

Select two or three of these contrasting examples of who Jesus is and what He did, and reflect on why this contrast is so important.

As disciples who want their influence to count, Jesus demonstrated for us that faithful service is accompanied by a willingness to be sacrificial. Jesus was obedient to His purpose, showing us that a willingness to sacrifice is the only way to have a lasting influence. After all, self-preservation never changed the world, just shrank it down until only one person mattered. Jesus blew it up so that everyone matters.

Today, spend some time in prayer reflecting on Jesus's sacrificial life. Ask Him to help you adopt His willingness to be sacrificial in your own life.

DAY 4
FOUR ADOPTABLE WAYS JESUS WAS HUMBLE

Vision: Jesus Embodied a Hopeful Vision Over Cynicism

> *For this reason, God highly exalted him and gave him the name that is above every name, so that at the name of Jesus every knee will bow—in heaven and on earth and under the earth—and every tongue will confess that Jesus Christ is Lord, to the glory of God the Father.*
> **PHILIPPIANS 2:9-11**

The humility of Jesus involved proximity to a rebellious people, the self-denial of His full glory, and radical obedience to the Father's will. All in all, He allowed himself to be humiliated: "He was like someone people turned away from; he was despised, and we didn't value him" (Isa. 53:3b). It is with the spirit of humility that Jesus fulfilled God's desired vision for redeeming humanity. Without humility, there would be no hopeful vision. And if that is true about our Lord, then it is expected of His followers.

We can know with absolute certainty that God will not allow a prideful person to experience the reward of leading and achieving a hope-filled vision. Why? Because God resists the proud (Prov. 3:34). And prideful people cannot lay aside their own wants and desires long enough to focus on what God wants. On the other hand, how amazing is it to humble ourselves and be used by God to lead a vision that achieves something extraordinary for the glory of God.

When have you seen a vision for the glory of God come together as a result of the willingness of people to humble themselves to the Lord's purposes?

When we closely examine Philippians 2:9-11, we find that the only way for us to capture the vision He has for humanity is to go ahead and kneel at His feet and humble ourselves before Him.

How can you kneel before Jesus today and humbly offer yourself to Him and for His purposes in the world?

It is a beautiful thing to behold a leader pursuing the highest good while clothed in a spirit of humility. It is a type of beauty that is difficult to describe, but when you see it, you know it. And when you experience it, you never forget it! One of the more rewarding aspects of the leadership journey is that God allows us to be creative when envisioning our future. He has blessed us with:

➤ An understanding of His desires and wants for His creation.

➤ An ability to create a vision for our lives in response to His desires.

➤ The greatest example to follow.

So, what is a hopeful vision that will consume your future? Once you have that figured out, choose every day to be generous, servant-minded, and sacrificial until the vision is completed. Do all this knowing that in the end, our reward is that "He will transform the body of our humble condition into the likeness of his glorious body, by the power that enables him to subject everything to himself" (Phil. 3:21).

> *Spend some time praying for the vision that God has for your life. You don't have to have it all figured out—just focus on today. Who does He want you to be as you seek to influence others for His kingdom and glory?*

SESSION 4

COUNTERCULTURAL SUCCESS

Session 4

VIDEO GUIDE

INTERVIEW: Anne Graham Lotz and Rachel-Ruth Wright

SCRIPTURE:

Therefore, my dear friends, just as you have always obeyed, so now, not only in my presence but even more in my absence, work out your own salvation with fear and trembling. For it is God who is working in you both to will and to work according to his good purpose. Do everything without grumbling and arguing, so that you may be blameless and pure, children of God who are faultless in a crooked and perverted generation, among whom you shine like stars in the world ...
PHILIPPIANS 2:12-15

NOTES:

INTERESTING QUOTE:

KEY POINTS:

Shine Like Stars in the World

Have you ever met someone so wounded that hope and happiness seemed more like a fairytale than an attainable reality? Maybe you've been there yourself, or maybe someone you love lives lost in the pain of a broken world.

I once met such a person while speaking at a student camp. One evening after the worship service everyone was outside looking at the stars. The reason hundreds of people were staring up at the sky was because on that night, two planets in our solar system were clearly visible. I think it was Jupiter and Venus, but don't hold me to it. I'm not a professional astronomer. In fact, if people had not pointed out which glowing dots in the sky were planets, I wouldn't have known the difference.

Everyone was looking up except one person. This seventh grader was just standing quietly in a sea of people fascinated with the beauty of the night sky. While everyone else was looking up, he was looking down. One of his group leaders noticed and asked why he wasn't looking up at the sky. He responded, "I don't look at the stars anymore. They just make me sad."

The two stepped aside and had a conversation. His mom and dad had divorced a couple of years earlier, and his dad had settled in with his "new family" just a few miles from his old one.

One of the favorite activities this young man had enjoyed with his dad was stargazing. In fact, his dad had purchased a telescope for them to look through and discover galaxies and constellations. But once the dust from the divorce settled, his dad came around less and less. Then one day, quite unceremoniously, the dad just stopped coming by to see his son altogether. Ever since then the telescope just sat in the corner of his room, a reminder of the dad he used to have, who now lived less than fifteen-minutes away but seemingly worlds apart.

It was a tough conversation. It involved a tough story and some tears. Eventually, through the love of an attentive group leader, shining brighter than the stars and planets in the sky that night, this broken boy heard some words of hope.

SUCCESSFUL INFLUENCE

The apostle Paul was acutely aware of just how messed up and broken our world is. After all, he had been a staunch enemy of the gospel and imprisoned men and women for following Jesus. That is why he wrote:

For it is God who is working in you both to will and to work according to his good purpose. Do everything without grumbling and arguing so that you may be blameless and pure, children of God who are faultless in a crooked and perverted generation, among whom you shine like stars in the world, by holding firm to the word of life.
PHILIPPIANS 2:13-15

A disciple of Jesus who wants to cultivate their influence shines like a star in a dark world so that God can accomplish His purposes through them. Of course, God's ultimate goal is that we would become "children of light" by walking in the marvelous light of Jesus (John 12:36). In John 8:12, Jesus said, "I am the light of the world. Anyone who follows me will never walk in the darkness but will have the light of life."

A COUNTERCULTURAL DEFINITION OF SUCCESS

When Paul wrote about shining like stars in the world, he was describing a disciple's influence. Still, it is an odd description. I mean, there are no actual stars in the world. Stars exist in the night sky; they illuminate the darkness capturing our attention and causing us to look up. From this layman's perspective, stars have one task and that is to shine bright.

In order to shine like stars we must learn to "do everything without grumbling and arguing" (Phil. 2:14). Unfortunately, in our world today, most people think shining is coming out on top of arguments. Whether in personal or online interactions, those labeled winners are often the ones who grumble the loudest or humiliate their opponent with the most personal insults.

> **How is it possible to shine in the world today without going down the road of personal insults, grumbling, and shouting matches?**

Because Jesus has given us life and the Holy Spirit is at work in us (Acts 1:8), we have everything necessary to illuminate every dark place in a world broken by sin. Therefore, as a disciple of Jesus, success means illuminating this world's darkness by accomplishing God's good purposes. This is a countercultural definition of success because it isn't focused on our personal brands, accumulating a lot of possessions, or having a big title.

How can a person live out this countercultural approach to success if they already have a lot of possessions or a big title?

Consider Philippians 2:13-15 again. We shine like stars in the world when:

➤ God's work in us motivates the kind of influence that accomplishes His purpose through us: "It is God who is working in you both to will and to work according to his good purpose" (v. 13).

➤ We live ethically according to the good work that Jesus has done in us: "Do everything without grumbling and arguing, so that you may be blameless and pure children of God" (vv. 14-15a).

➤ We give people hope because of the message that gave us life: "Faultless in a crooked and perverted generation, among whom you shine like stars in the world, by holding firm to the word of life" (vv. 15b-16).

We have the responsibility to apply our salvation to every part of our lives. As we do, God works in us and through us so that we may shine like stars in the world. This is the type of influence that Paul wanted for the disciples in Philippi, and this is the type of leadership that God still desires for His sons and daughters to practice today.

It is a sad reality, but we live in a world where a middle schooler won't look up at the stars because his broken heart is too heavy. Thank God for a group leader who was sensitive enough to realize the pain that was far heavier than any seventh grader should ever have to carry. A leader who was motivated by Jesus to be transparent and authentic—showing and sharing the only message that could bring hope and life. On a summer evening where hundreds of people were looking up, the brightest star shined there on the ground. It was a countercultural understanding of success, but it was the kind of influence that pleases the heart of God.

Discussion Questions

How have you seen God working His good purpose in you? How can you know if what is happening in your life is according to God's good purpose?

Why is it counter productive to grumble and argue? When have you seen someone shine like a star in the world without grumbling or arguing?

When you live blameless and pure, you stand in sharp contrast to the world. How did Jesus display these characteristics in His interactions with others?

How do you hold firm to the word of life?

How can you use whatever presence you have online to shine like a star in the world and hold firm to the word of life?

Someone who is countercultural does things the opposite of everyone else. On a separate piece of paper, write 3-4 sentences on someone who is countercultural. What makes them countercultural? Remember that being different for the sake of the gospel is the goal, not for the sake of being different.

DAY 1
FOUR WAYS TO SHINE

The Unfortunately Overlooked, Mildly Misunderstood, Significance of "Fear and Trembling"

Work out your own salvation with fear and trembling.
PHILIPPIANS 2:12b

With just our English understanding of words, we could easily conclude this verse to mean we must be very afraid and to use that fear to motivate us to work and serve God, so that we don't lose our salvation. With the logic being that if we are always afraid of losing something, then we never will, right? This couldn't be any more wrong!

Now take a deep breath, and let's evaluate this verse on a deeper level. First, we need to understand three terms. *Work out* means to continuously work hard at a task or goal until it is carried out to completion. *Fear* means to have reverence or a consuming sense of awe. *Trembling* is where we get our English word "tremor" from. In this context, it means shaking with nervous excitement due to consuming awe and reverence.

With these definitions and understanding, rewrite Philippians 2:12b in your own words.

Now let's interpret and apply this verse to our lives and leadership. We work out our salvation by choosing to exhaustively apply it to every part of our lives. Because we are redeemed, Jesus is relevant to every area of life. We work out our salvation with astonishment and awe that, at times, is overwhelming. If we have experienced the miracle of being brought from spiritual death to life, then being astonished and overwhelmed aren't too difficult to imagine.

Working out our salvation is much like exercising or working out. In order to grow stronger, we must keep after it. List three ways you can keep working out your salvation—not in order to keep it—but in order to grow stronger in it.

Have you ever known someone who met a celebrity they deeply admired only to have their emotions get the best of them? In an unhealthy way, that's fear and trembling. They were simply in awe, and their emotions showed it with tears and shaking and breathlessness. As disciples of Jesus, we get so much more than a chance meeting and heightened emotions. The most honored being ever (and by the way, this type of honor is only reserved for Jesus) has said to us, "Come and follow me."

Now, what does this have to do with influence? If we can't work out our own salvation, how can our lives be an example to others? If we aren't more and more in awe of Jesus and experiencing moments where the weight of our emotions seems to grip our hearts, then how can we give hope to others?

> *Close this time in prayer asking God to give you the correct sense of awe and respect for Jesus that He deserves. Then spend a few moments just focusing your every thought on how wonderful and glorious He is.*

DAY 2
FOUR WAYS TO SHINE

The Sound of Failing Leadership

Do everything without grumbling or arguing ...
PHILIPPIANS 2:14

Like yesterday, a little understanding of the original biblical language can go a long way. It's going to be helpful today, but in a different way. In most languages, there are onomatopoetic words. Now let's be honest, most of us (including myself) aren't that familiar with the word *onomatopoetic*. It is a word that when spoken, sounds like the object or event that it is describing. For example, the word *buzz* sounds like buzzing, and the word *achoo* sounds like a sneeze.

In verse 12, the apostle Paul encouraged the Philippian Christians to work out their salvation, allowing God to work in and through them to accomplish His good purposes. Immediately following this, he instructed them to do everything without grumbling and arguing. The word *grumbling* is associated with people complaining amongst themselves in an open area like a lobby or courtyard. If you stand back and listen to a group of people murmuring amongst themselves, it sounds like the cooing of doves (which gives the word it's onomatopoetic quality). The second word he used is *arguing,* which implies getting into disputes over opinions.[2]

Take a moment and think about the last argument you were in. Were you able to convince the person you were arguing with that you were right? Did they change your mind? What is your lasting impression of the argument?

Session 4

It is safe to say that our society is filled with noise. There is more opportunity for one to voice an opinion or thought than at any other time in human history. The technological age we live in with all of its platforms and possibilities deserves the credit for making this historical phenomenon achievable. Nevertheless, there is a caution we must all be aware of, a temptation continually seeking to draw us into a destructive trap. It is the idea that I am entitled to have my opinions heard and even argued about. To all of this, Paul called us to rise above the noise so that we can shine like stars in the world.

What steps can you take to discern which opinions you should share and which ones you should disregard?

How can you disagree with someone's opinion while still holding on to the truth of God's Word?

For the disciple who wants to influence, it is difficult to shine bright while complaining and even harder still when arguing over matters of opinion. Because leadership begins at the feet of Jesus, we have given up our rights in service to His purposes. So fight against the tide of cultural entitlements that lead us to complain and quarrel. After all, it's difficult to have a voice that stands out if all of our energy is only contributing to the soundtrack of noise. The sound of failing leadership can be heard among the grumblers and gripers, the contentious contenders of entitlements and opinions.

> *Today, pray that God would help you not be mired in the noise.*
> *Ask Him to help you strive to shine by not grumbling or arguing.*

DAY 3
FOUR WAYS TO SHINE

A Rhythm of Challenging the Process: The Three Most Important Questions Successful Leaders Ask

Shine like stars in the world, by holding firm to the word of life.
PHILIPPIANS 2:15-16

We will never maximize the full potential of our leadership if we are continually aiming at the status quo. There must be a rhythm by which we challenge our leadership process if we are to continually grow in our ability to influence. One of the most important research projects on the subject was conducted by two professors attempting to understand the best practices of leaders. Essentially, they discovered that there are five practices of exemplary leadership: model the way, inspire a shared vision, challenge the process, enable others to act, and encourage the heart.[1]

Many leaders struggle with the third practice of challenging the process. Yet it is essential, not just for companies that make products, but for disciples who want to lead like Jesus. Don't believe me? Notice throughout the Gospels how often Jesus challenged the process of the religious leaders of His day.

How do disciples challenge the process to improve and grow? Fortunately, Paul answered the question for us in saying, "by holding firm to the word of life" (Phil 2:16). The word of life is the gospel message and the teachings of Scripture. We can understand it this way: the more we grow in our relationship with Jesus, the more we will learn about following Jesus, leading to a deeper understand of how to live and lead the way Jesus did. I believe three questions help us challenge the process:

1. **HEALTH:** Am I aware of how God is at work in and through me?
2. **TALENT:** Have I identified and am I living out the gifts, skills, and talents that God has given me?

3. **VISION:** Am I pursuing a vision with my life that illuminates the dark places in this broken world?

Knowing that we are supposed to challenge the process and having the right questions to ask isn't enough. We must choose to create a rhythm that helps us shine like stars in the world by allowing others to speak into our lives. We must also always cling tightly to the word of life.

Let's take inventory and challenge the process of your leadership. Answer the following questions:

AM I HEALTHY: Do I allow others to hold me accountable for my actions in how I hold firmly to the word of life?

WHAT ARE MY TALENTS: Am I using the gifts and abilities God has given me for good and for His glory?

WHAT IS THE VISION OF MY LIFE: Am I living in such a way that lights up the dark places and helps heal the broken?

> *Today in your time of prayer, dwell on the phrase "holding firm to the word of life." Ask God to show you places where you are not holding firm and seek to tighten your grip on Him, His Word, and the life He offers you.*

DAY 4
FOUR WAYS TO SHINE

The Feeling of Countercultural Success

Then I can boast in the day of Christ that I didn't run or labor for nothing. But even if I am poured out as a drink offering on the sacrificial service of your faith, I am glad and rejoice with all of you. In the same way, you should also be glad and rejoice with me.
PHILIPPIANS 2:16b-18

A disciple of Jesus will always measure their success differently from leaders who are not motivated by the love and desires of God. And so, their feeling of success will be countercultural. As Paul ended this focus on disciples shining like stars in the world, he expressed an emotion that occurs when a leader's sole motivation is to please Christ: *joy*. Paul eagerly anticipated that moment when he would rejoice in the presence of Jesus, even if it meant suffering ("being poured out") in the present.

When have you felt "poured out" as a result of serving God?

Furthermore, his present sufferings and service were also reasons to rejoice. Why? Because all of his labors were in "sacrificial service" for the faith of the Philippian Christians. If he emptied himself and gave his life in service to people so that they could tell a redemptive story with their lives, then Paul viewed that as worth it and a life well-lived.

We live in a culture where success is defined differently. Our world says, "to the victor goes the spoils." This is the idea that being a successful leader is rewarded with the benefits of success. Usually, that means money, status, power, and so on.

It's a hollow reward in the end. It's success that yields temporary pleasures, but never fully satisfies the eternal soul.

When have you heard about someone who was very successful by the world's standards, but confessed to feeling empty on the inside?

A disclaimer: I know many people who have been incredibly successful in business, the arts, education, and more. They have made lots of money, built large companies, and could purchase just about anything their minds could imagine. Yet, they do not see these things as anything more than tools to be used for a larger purpose. That is because their ultimate success is found in lighting up the dark. Therefore, they rejoice when people are impacted according to God's good purposes. Everything else is just a resource for the story that God is telling in and through their lives. Disclaimer over.

If we choose to view success through the lens of God's purposes, then we're going to measure success in a totally different way than the world does. But, on the flip side, we get to partake in a joy that lasts forever. When our ambitions are redeemed and success is redefined, we live and lead surrendered to what God wants. This offers us joy in the present and joy in the future.

As children of God, we are privileged people. First, there is a real day on God's calendar when we will see Him face to face and get the privilege of sharing in our Savior's joy (Matt. 25:21,23). Second, we can spend our lives confidently anticipating the eternal impact of pursuing a gospel-motivated version of success. People who are successful in God's eyes get to have joy both today and joy forever.

> *Pray today that God will define for you what success is. If you are stuck thinking in a worldly pattern of what success looks like, ask God to redefine it for you. Meditate on Paul's words in Philippians 2:16b-17. Then filter success through that lens.*

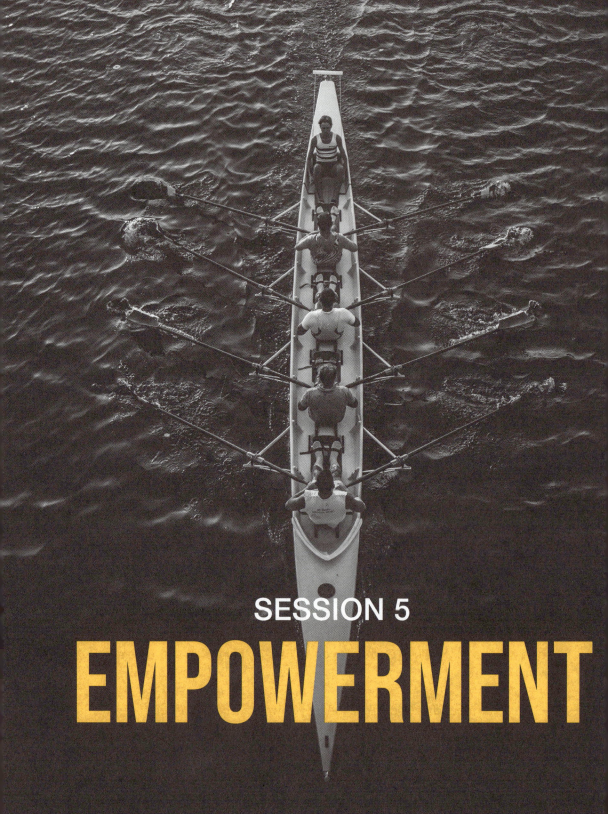

Session 5

VIDEO GUIDE

INTERVIEW: Dr. Michael Catt

SCRIPTURE:

Now I hope in the Lord Jesus to send Timothy to you soon so that I too may be encouraged by news about you. For I have no one else like-minded who will genuinely care about your interests; all seek their own interests, not those of Jesus Christ. But you know his proven character, because he has served with me in the gospel ministry like a son with a father. Therefore, I hope to send him as soon as I see how things go with me. I am confident in the Lord that I myself will also come soon. But I considered it necessary to send you Epaphroditus—my brother, coworker, and fellow soldier, as well as your messenger and minister to my need ...
PHILIPPIANS 2:19-25

NOTES:

INTERESTING QUOTE:

KEY POINTS:

"Go On, in the Name of God"

John Wesley lived to be 88 years old, a very long time for a man in the eighteenth century. And what a life it was! Known for being one of England's most important spiritual leaders, he led a spiritual awakening movement that impacted much of eighteenth-century culture. Let's just say he was a leader that didn't have an off switch:

- Over the course of 54 years, he averaged three sermons a day, preaching almost 45,000 times.[1]

- Long before the Honda Accord, he traveled by horseback and carriage, logging more than 200,000 miles and averaging 5,000 miles a year.[2]

- He trained over 2,000 ministry leaders.[3]

- And he wrote a four-volume Bible commentary, an English dictionary, multiple books on philosophy and church history, works on the history of England and Rome, papers on medicine, six volumes on church music, and seven books filled with sermons and papers.[4]

An untold number of people came to faith in Christ under his preaching and teaching. But 230 years after he stepped foot into heaven, one of the most important aspects of his ministry was his unwavering conviction that slavery was evil. As he approached the final years of his life, he read about a young politician named William Wilberforce, an outspoken Christian who also wanted to see an end to slavery. The last letter Wesley ever wrote was to Wilberforce. This is a portion of that final correspondence:

> Dear Sir:
>
> Unless the divine power has raised you up … I see not how you can go through your glorious enterprise in opposing that execrable villainy, which is the scandal of religion, of England, and of human nature. Unless God has raised you up for this very thing, you will be worn out by the opposition of men and devils. But if God be for you, who can be against you? Are all of them stronger than God? O be not weary of well-doing! Go on, in the name of God and in the power of his might, till even American slavery (the vilest that ever saw the sun) shall vanish away before it.[5]

Hours after writing this letter, Wesley slipped into a coma, and a few short days later, passed from earth to glory.

Wilberforce fought against slavery all of his life. By the grace of God, just three days before his death in 1833, the slave trade was abolished and all slaves emancipated across the whole British Empire. It is said that Wilberforce kept the letter Wesley wrote to him in the pages of his Bible, where he would see it often.

BELIEVING IN AND EMPOWERING

John Wesley spent his final moments believing in and empowering a young leader he had never personally met. There is something incredibly inspiring about a leader who empowers others to fulfill a vision. Wesley did it, and so did the apostle Paul writing his last letter to Timothy from a Roman prison just before he was to be executed (2 Tim.).

Paul was a leader that believed in helping younger leaders find their voices and receive opportunities to exercise their gifts. This is why he empowered two men to serve the Philippians while imprisoned. First, he mentioned Timothy, a young man he discipled and whom he viewed as a son. Secondly, he mentioned Epaphroditus, a Philippian believer who had served in bringing gifts from the church to Paul in Rome, had nearly died from a sickness, and now had delivered this letter back to the church.

Who is a leader that has believed in you?

How has he or she empowered you?

What life lesson has this leader taught you that you will always remember and pass on to others?

How have they challenged you to "go on, in the name of God"?

PHILIPPIANS

Concerning Timothy, Paul wrote:

> *Now I hope in the Lord Jesus to send Timothy to you soon so that I too may be encouraged by news about you. For I have no one else like-minded who will genuinely care about your interests; all seek their own interests, not those of Jesus Christ. But you know his proven character because he has served with me in the gospel ministry like a son with a father. Therefore, I hope to send him as soon as I see how things go with me. I am confident in the Lord that I myself will also come soon.*
>
> **PHILIPPIANS 2:19-24**

In Philippians 2:19-24, Paul's belief in Timothy was on full display. The question now is, how does a leader empower others to go on in the name of God? A closer look at these verses will reveal a clear pathway:

➤ Celebrate the leader's strengths: "I have no one else like-minded who will genuinely care about your interests" (v. 20).

➤ Emphasize how the leader has genuinely served: "Who will genuinely care about your interests; all seek their own interests, not those of Jesus Christ" (v. 20b-21).

➤ Build up the leader by validating her or his character: "You know his proven character because he has served with me in gospel ministry" (v. 22).

➤ Vouch for the leader's reputation: "You know his proven character because he has served with me in gospel ministry" (v. 22).

➤ Refer to the leader in loving terms that validate trust and confidence: "He has served with me in the gospel ministry like a son with a father" (v. 22).

In order for a mentor to do these things for you, they have to be true. Paul knew that Timothy exhibited these qualities (and more) because they served side by side. These qualities have to be nurtured and developed over time. It doesn't happen quickly, but as you walk with the Spirit, He develops strengths and character, and a reputation in you becomes evident not only to those that love you, but to the watching world as well.

Discussion Questions

John Wesley and William Wilberforce dedicated their lives to serving the Lord, first through sharing the gospel with others and also seeking the end of the abhorrent slave trade. What can you pour yourself into that both honors Christ and serves others?

What would you say your strengths are? How about your weaknesses? How can you improve on your weaknesses?

When has been a time when you have genuinely served, looking out for the interests of others over your own?

How do we grown in our character? What steps should we take when we've had a setback in our desire to be a person of character, or if we don't currently have a strong reputation?

What are two things you can do now as a young leader that will help gain the trust of your parents, mentors, and leaders in your life?

Even as a young leader, how can you believe in and empower others?

DAY 1
THE SYMPHONY OF EMPOWERMENT

Brother: "I Value You"

*But I considered it necessary to send you Epaphroditus—
my brother, coworker, and fellow soldier, as well as
your messenger and minister to my need ...*
PHILIPPIANS 2:25

Believing in someone else to accomplish a task or vision is one of the most significant things a leader can do. Energy spent empowering others is never wasted. This is what Paul accomplished with Epaphroditus. In one sentence, he masterfully showed us the progression of how he built up and empowered the man from Philippi. He uses four edifying words, each making a statement and each creating a sense of momentum from one description to the next. In fact, the type of words used are like a symphony that builds and builds towards a crescendo. The first word Paul used was *brother,* which in Greek means literally, "from the same womb."[6] This is a picture of two men who share a common origin and share a common standing.

> **Who in your life feels as close to you as a brother or sister? How did your relationship grow so close?**

Paul loved and esteemed Epaphroditus as if he were family. It's a beautiful picture of what the gospel can accomplish. One man had been a Pharisee; the other was a Gentile. In his previous life, Paul would have looked down upon Epaphroditus. Now, he looked at him through the lens of redemption. They had both been orphaned by sin, and Jesus had adopted them into the same family. The gospel doesn't just make enemies friends or simply help people get along who formerly had nothing to do with each other. The gospel makes us family. Paul was a child of God and viewed Epaphroditus as his brother. They had both been equally lost, just in different ways, but Jesus brought them out of the lonely wilderness of their own making. Now they were standing on level ground as equals and brothers.

Describe how the gospel has transformed you.

Describe a time when the gospel transformed someone who is very different from you into the same redemption you've found in Jesus.

When we realize that God has redeemed us, we get to discover and celebrate the value of others who have been redeemed. Paul couldn't see worth and value in Epaphroditus in his previous life, but now he had eyes to see and his heart was full of gratitude for his brother.

Empowering people means helping them feel inspired and authorized to think, dream, and lead at the feet of Jesus. It is a powerful and God-honoring way to steward one's influence. But it begins with the idea that we all kneel on equal ground at the foot of the cross. After all, "In Christ, there is not Greek and Jew, circumcision and uncircumcision, barbarian, Scythian, slave and free; but Christ is all and in all" (Col. 3:11). Therefore, Paul's first description of Epaphroditus communicated, "I value you as my brother in Christ."

> *Pray today that God would help you value your brothers and sisters in Christ. Ask Him to help you see that you all stand on equal footing at the cross and have been saved by the same redemption in Christ.*

DAY 2
THE SYMPHONY OF EMPOWERMENT

Coworker: "I Respect You"

*But I considered it necessary to send you Epaphroditus—
my brother, coworker, and fellow soldier, as well as
your messenger and minister to my need ...*

PHILIPPIANS 2:25

The symphony of empowerment Paul created as he described Epaphroditus continued to build and swell with the following description: coworker. The two men had labored together in gospel ministry. Paul now used the word *coworker* to express how they served together as friends and not in an impersonal work relationship where they had little concern for each other. As with the other acclamations, Paul placed himself on equal and common ground with his brother and coworker.

Describe a time when you worked alongside someone else, such as on a mission trip or a project for school.

How has working alongside someone else drawn you closer to that person?

Leaders often feel the need to jump out front, being loud and boisterous and giving directions that only communicate, "follow me!" Yet Paul took a countercultural approach to leadership: he influenced while walking side by side instead of jumping out in front. By walking next to Epaphroditus and laboring with him, he communicated: "I respect you."

Respect means to hold someone in high regard, to admire, and have honor for such a person. Paul encouraged us to "love one another deeply as brothers and sisters. Take the lead in honoring one another" (Rom. 12:10). When we love, we position ourselves to show respect. When we honor another, we demonstrate our respect. Healthy leaders aren't afraid to build others up. They aren't overly concerned with their "brand," which is often just our feeble attempt to mask insecurity. No, they take joy when others succeed and rejoice when God uses others in an even more powerful way than He used them. All of this is possible in the leader's life because they see the value and respect others.

Who is a person you respect? How did you grow to respect that person?

Think about it this way: Vision is never accomplished in a vacuum, and leaders do not lead in a silo. The Lord allows our hearts and minds to be motivated to change the world in different ways. Therefore, leaders are not all the same. To accomplish a vision by influencing others to galvanize around a cause, project, or company means the leader has to see the profound value in others and regard them with a sacred sense of respect. Commit to being the leader that respects, walks beside, and labors shoulder to shoulder with others. When we respect those the Lord brings into our lives, we empower them to accomplish the task at hand and to believe that they could be further used according to the redemptive purposes of God.

> *Think about the people in your church, student ministry, or small group. Take some time to pray today that God would lead your hearts to respect each other as coworkers in the gospel. Pray that He would be the unifying force you all share in common.*

DAY 3
THE SYMPHONY OF EMPOWERMENT

Fellow Soldier: "I've Got Your Back"

> *But I considered it necessary to send you Epaphroditus— my brother, coworker, and fellow soldier, as well as your messenger and minister to my need ...*
> **PHILIPPIANS 2:25**

As the symphony of empowerment continues to build momentum, Epaphroditus is described as a fellow soldier. The phrase also translates to *fellow struggler* and means "one who serves in arduous tasks or undergoes severe experiences together with someone else."[7]

Both Paul and Epaphroditus had undergone harrowing experiences in their ministries. Paul even explained how his fellow struggler had been "so sick that he nearly died" (v. 27). In writing to the church in Philippi, he wanted the entire city to know that Epaphroditus had been fighting the good fight (2 Tim. 4:7). Leaders who empower others are willing to struggle and endure with others. You see, when we have each other's back, it only makes us both stronger.

Who is someone in your life that you know, beyond a shadow of a doubt, has your back?

How did this trust form?

The fight we are engaged in is sometimes a physical struggle and sometimes a spiritual one. But always remember, the battle is sacred because we are sharing in the work of Christ.

Paul described the struggle in Ephesians 6:12:

> *For our struggle is not against flesh and blood, but against the rulers, against the authorities, against the cosmic powers of this darkness, against evil, spiritual forces in the heavens.*
> **EPHESIANS 6:12**

How have you struggled together with other believers in this fight against the powers of darkness and evil?

The battle rages on in this broken world. Quite simply put, it is a war between good and evil, between God and Satan's evil forces that oppose Him. It is a war for the souls of men and women and the fulfillment of God's mission. While the end has already been determined and victory is just a matter of time away, we must continue fighting in the present. We fight in the name of Jesus and under the banner of His redemption, lighting up the dark by taking an active part in God's objective. When will the battle conclude? The date is not for us to know. Our responsibility is to fight on with our fellow soldiers, having each other's backs until God calls us into the glorious ever after.

How can you have the backs of the fellow soldiers in your life?

> *Close this time praying for a desire to have the back of the fellow soldiers in your life. Also pray that they would have your back as you seek to serve God together and influence others.*

DAY 4
THE SYMPHONY OF EMPOWERMENT

Messenger: "I Trust You"

*But I considered it necessary to send you Epaphroditus—
my brother, coworker, and fellow soldier, as well as
your messenger and minister to my need ...*
PHILIPPIANS 2:25

A symphony typically has four parts which are called movements. Each movement stands alone, and there is a pause before the next movement begins. Each movement is part of the whole. The four movements to Paul's symphonic description are:

➤ "I value you."

➤ "I respect you."

➤ "I have your back."

➤ "I trust you."

Each movement gives way to the next so that when the final part of the symphony is understood, the listener is left knowing that the sum is greater than the parts. In the case of Paul's words concerning Epaphroditus, the sum total equals empowerment.

What makes you feel empowered?

The final movement of Paul's symphony of empowerment is messenger. The word *messenger*—now wait for genius—simply means someone who is sent with a message.[8] Okay, so it's a word that is easy to understand. But let's be honest: sending a person out with a vision, message, and significant responsibility can be very difficult because it involves trust. Most scholars believe that Paul trusted Epaphroditus with the letter to the Philippians; the very book of Philippians that appears in your Bible! This is a mammoth task that involves trust that only comes when the leader values, respects, and has the individual's back.

What is a task that someone has entrusted to you?

How did they empower you to complete the task?

Trust involves fully believing the best about others. The world needs a few more leaders who believe in and rejoice in the capacity and potential of others. Believing that any success for the wants of God is a victory we all can share in. This is the beautiful thing about those who truly empower others—their applause for others gets louder, not quieter, with the passing of time. Paul showed us in how he spoke of Epaphroditus that his applause began sitting down, but ended with a standing ovation.

In a world where so much focus is on building up the self, empower others to envision what could and should be. Then believe in them as they pursue what pleases God. Only the rare type of leader can influence in this manner. Consider this: when you construct a symphony of empowerment for someone, you are replicating what Jesus has accomplished in you and that is a leadership journey well taken.

> *Ask God to help you choose to be a leader whose belief in others is a symphony of empowerment.*

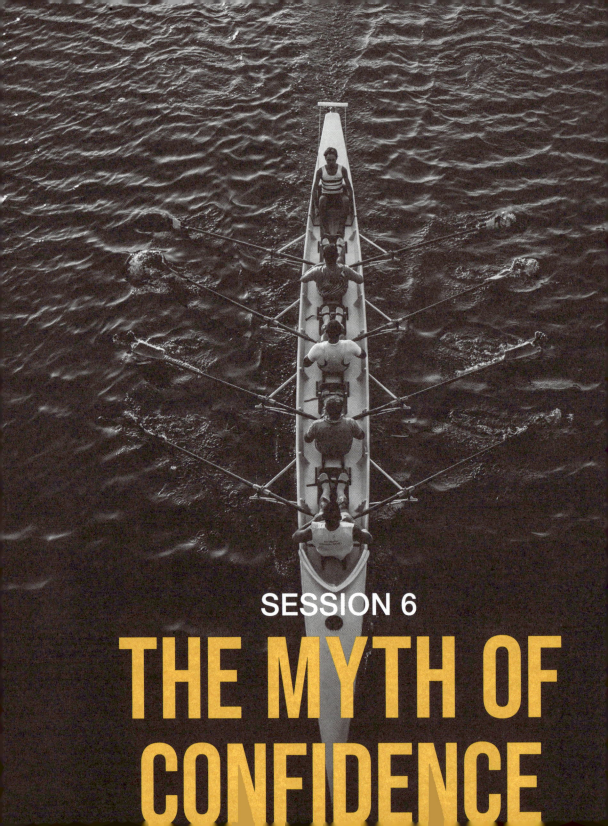

SESSION 6

THE MYTH OF CONFIDENCE

VIDEO GUIDE

INTERVIEW: Wendy Wright

SCRIPTURE:

My goal is to know him and the power of his resurrection and the fellowship of his sufferings, being conformed to his death, assuming that I will somehow reach the resurrection from among the dead.
PHILIPPIANS 3:10-11

NOTES:

INTERESTING QUOTE:

KEY POINTS:

Purpose

A famous sports writer named Rick Reilly once wrote a story about the oddest game in high school football history. It was played in 2008, in Grapevine, Texas, between the Faith Lions and the Gainesville Tornadoes.[1] It was a game played like any other, but this would not be a typical Friday night lights showdown. The Faith Lions represented a prominent Christian school that had over seventy players, a full coaching staff, and the best equipment available. The Gainesville Tornadoes came from a maximum-security correctional facility with old equipment and were escorted on and off the field by armed police officers.

The reason they played that night came down to one man's purpose. In a state where the Friday night lights burn bright and victory or defeat means everything, purpose turned the normal scoreboard upside down. Kris Hogan, the head coach for the Lions, had heard about the Tornadoes and wanted to find a tangible way to express God's love to them.

Coach Hogan came up with the craziest idea a head football coach could ever conceive. He asked half of the Lions' fans to sit in the visitor's section and cheer for the other team for one night. When the Tornadoes came out of the locker room, the Lions' fans made a spirit tunnel for them to run through. Then throughout the entire game, a sea of people cheered them on. Reilly described it as, "rivers running uphill and cats petting dogs. More than 200 Faith fans sat on the Gainesville side and kept cheering the Gainesville players on—by name."[2]

Coach Hogan is a man of great faith who knows his purpose: "But one thing I do: Forgetting what is behind and reaching forward to what is ahead, I pursue as my goal the prize promised by God's heavenly call in Christ Jesus" (Phil. 3:13-14).

They play a lot of football in Texas, and most of the time, what's on the scoreboard at the end of the game is all that matters. But one night, years ago, a coach who knows his purpose decided to demonstrate it to a bunch of young men who had been defined by their worst moments. On what would have been a night long forgotten, the story is still told of a coach, some fans, and a team who wanted to say, "You are just as valuable as anyone else, and you are deeply loved." You see, someone consumed with knowing Jesus is positioned to influence others for Jesus.

CONFIDENCE VS. PURPOSE

Unless we have a purpose for our lives, it doesn't really matter how strong our leadership qualities are. For Paul, leadership was less about confidence and more about his purpose—knowing God.

> *I have reasons for confidence in the flesh. If anyone else thinks he has grounds for confidence in the flesh, I have more: circumcised the eighth day; of the nation of Israel, of the tribe of Benjamin, a Hebrew born of Hebrews; regarding the law, a Pharisee; regarding zeal, persecuting the church; regarding the righteousness that is in the law, blameless. But everything that was a gain to me, I have considered to be a loss because of Christ. More than that, I also consider everything to be a loss in view of the surpassing value of knowing Christ Jesus my Lord. Because of him I have suffered the loss of all things and consider them as dung, so that I may gain Christ and be found in him, not having a righteousness of my own from the law, but one that is through faith in Christ—the righteousness from God based on faith. My goal is to know him and the power of his resurrection and the fellowship of his sufferings, being conformed to his death, assuming that I will somehow reach the resurrection from among the dead.*
> **PHILIPPIANS 3:4-11**

These verses can be divided into two ideas:

1. Philippians 3:4-6: Paul's confidence in himself, his own human effort, and his accomplishments.
2. Philippians 3: 7-11: Paul's purpose of knowing and experiencing Jesus.

What would you say is your purpose in life?

There is an invaluable lesson to be learned here for all disciples wanting to use their influence for the glory of God:

First: Your leadership is pointless if it is a story about your personal platform, where you confidently and constantly parade out your own accomplishments.

Second: You will position your life to influence for Jesus only when your purpose is to be consumed with knowing Him.

PHILIPPIANS

Let's unpack Paul's original misguided overconfident approach to leadership that in the end was a house of cards that came crumbling down (see Acts 9:1-25). What does misguided confidence look like?

➤ Confidence in a pedigree or position: "circumcised the eighth day; of the nation of Israel, of the tribe of Benjamin, a Hebrew born of Hebrews" (Phil 3:5).

➤ Confidence in personal accomplishment: "regarding the law, a Pharisee … regarding the righteousness that is in the law, blameless" (vv. 5-6).

➤ Confident to take action against any threat: "regarding zeal, persecuting the church" (v. 6).

In his former life, Paul found his confidence in being born into the right family, following all the rules, and attacking those who threatened him. In modern terms, Paul had built his brand on genealogy, accomplishment, and activism. By today's standards, he would have been considered an influencer worthy of following and imitating. But there's just one problem: Paul was the hero of his own story.

How does being the hero of our own story always end up falling short in the end?

Thankfully, the story doesn't end with Paul's misguided confidence. Instead, the story of his influence began where his confidence ended and his purpose was discovered. You see, all of Paul's influence derived from his purpose: "My goal is to know him" (Phil. 3:10). This is why over and over again we must remind ourselves that leadership begins at the feet of Jesus. Our goal should always be to know Him and to be consumed with knowing Him. We should be so consumed that nothing else has meaning apart from "the surpassing value of knowing Christ Jesus my Lord" (v. 8). When we consume ourselves with knowing Jesus, our minds and hearts prioritize what matters to Jesus. And that is where we discover Christ-honoring influence.

Discussion Questions

What are some present-day examples of misplaced confidence?

What are some of the consequences of misplaced confidence? (For the apostle Paul this would be his persecution of the church.)

Does knowing our purpose mean we discard and ignore our gifts and talents? How does our purpose redefine our gifts and talents? (Think back to the example of Coach Hogan and the Faith Lions.)

Take a few moments and identify historic or contemporary leaders who have used their talents, gifts, positions, and status as an expression of their ultimate purpose in life.

Paul originally rested his confidence on his heritage and accomplishments. What are some things people use today to build up their own confidence?

What has to happen in your own life for everything to be considered loss compared to knowing Jesus?

DAY 1
FOUR QUESTIONS, ONE PURPOSE

"How Will I Think?"

> *But everything that was a gain to me, I have considered to be a loss because of Christ.*
> **PHILIPPIANS 3:7**

There is a series of questions that shape and reveal the purpose at the center of our lives. They are simple questions, but that doesn't mean they are easy. Honestly, each one can lead to a lifetime of reflection and purpose. All four questions create a code of living that helps cultivate clarity in both the small and big moments of life.

What questions, up until now, have you asked yourself when you needed to make a decision?

The first question focuses on our mindset: "How will I think?" It is a question designed to help focus our minds and prevent us from thinking in an unhealthy manner. Simply put, if we fail to think correctly about ourselves, then we will deceive ourselves. Paul wrote in Galatians 6:3, "For if anyone considers himself to be something when he is nothing, he deceives himself." The deception he is writing about is a mental deception. The type of influence worthy of a citizen of heaven must begin with right thinking.

How have you been deceived in your thinking about yourself in the past?

This is why Paul conveyed in the strongest terms possible that a religious resume is nothing but a house of cards (Phil. 3:4-7). All that he thought was important — coming from a respected family, wealthy upbringing, prestigious education, flawless living, and religious activity — was lost in a moment. Everything that made Paul an influencer in his culture was instantaneously reduced to nothingness in one single, life-altering event. When the light of Jesus shone down from heaven, it evaporated Paul's resume, and all that remained was a blind man who could now see. Furthermore, the most amazing leader in the history of the church decided to live the rest of his life based on that one moment in time. It determined how he thought about himself and how he managed his influence.

When you "saw the light" and came to faith in Christ, how did He change your mindset about yourself?

It is incredible how redemption grants a perspective that should have seemed so obvious. We can spend a lifetime chasing everything that glitters without realizing it's not gold. And then the moment we become sons and daughters of God, it's as if we see for the very first time. The challenge for all of us is to live in that moment — to maintain a mindset more spellbound with the grace of Jesus at the dawning of each day.

> *As you pray today, ask God to shape your mindset. Ask Him to reveal where you have been or are deceived in your thinking. Ask Him to change your mind to see yourself in the right light and to filter everything through the lens of your salvation, not through the way the world sees.*

DAY 2
FOUR QUESTIONS, ONE PURPOSE

"What Do I Value?"

I also consider everything to be a loss in view of the surpassing value of knowing Christ Jesus my Lord.
PHILIPPIANS 3:8a

The second question focuses on what matters to us. In other words, what holds value in our lives. Paul was no longer the shining star of the Sanhedrin. After coming to faith in Christ, he was a star in the world shining the light of Jesus. His former resume won him no acclaim: now he based everything on knowing Jesus. It is not a hyperbole for him to describe how he considered everything to be a loss compared to knowing Jesus. Paul was demonstrating to the believers in Philippi that nothing can in any measurable way compare in value to the intimate experience of communion with God.

List three ways have you found communion with God valuable throughout your relationship with Him:

Paul's leadership teaches us to value what God can accomplish. The verses in Philippians 3:9-11 have served for much of church history as a guide for church leaders to teach about placing a high value on what only God can accomplish.

WHAT CAN GOD ACCOMPLISH?

JUSTIFICATION: Christ has forgiven us and given us a right standing with God.

> *Be found in him, not having a righteousness of my own from the law, but one that is through faith in Christ— the righteousness from God based on faith.*
> **PHILIPPIANS 3:9**

SANCTIFICATION: Christ is at work in our lives.

> *My goal is to know him and the power of his resurrection and the fellowship of his sufferings, being conformed to His death ...*
> **PHILIPPIANS 3:10**

GLORIFICATION: God will complete the good work He began in us.

> *... assuming that I will somehow reach the resurrection from among the dead.*
> **PHILIPPIANS 3:11**

To sum it all up, value what only God can accomplish. How is this important to leadership? Because the person who daily values God's accomplishments will never fall into the trap of pride and self-sufficiency (Isa. 2:11).

Pray that God would bring these three things to your mind throughout the day. Be reminded that you have been justified— forgiven from all your sins, past and present. Remember that God is sanctifying you, transforming you into the likeness of Jesus daily as you walk with Him. Finally, remember that one day in the future, you will be glorified. Not in the way that Jesus is glorified, but in that your time on earth will be complete and you will finally have your forever reward, an eternity in heaven.

DAY 3
FOUR QUESTIONS, ONE PURPOSE

"What Am I Willing to Lose?"

Because of him I have suffered the loss of all things and consider them as dung, so that I may gain Christ ...
PHILIPPIANS 3:8b

You can tell a lot about someone by what they are willing to lose or how tightly they hold onto things. In just two sentences (vv. 7-8), Paul uses the word "loss" three times! He also uses the word "gain" a couple of times. Both are marketplace terms that had to do with profits and losses on goods traded or sold. It is a fascinating paradigm. In the end, all of the assets that were so valuable to Paul as a religious leader were a mountain of debt, and the only way to get out of debt was to gain Christ.

Consider what you have lost by following Jesus and what you have gained. List things lost and gained in the chart below:

LOST	GAINED

It cannot be stressed enough and is a countercultural perspective, but it is only when we are willing to lose all that we thought mattered that we discover what truly matters. In a world that places a high value on social platforms and branding, God is looking for those who are willing to lose it all to gain Christ.

In following Christ, you may not lose your social media status, reputation for being a creative thought leader, or your social status among other students. But you must be *willing* to lose all of those things to gain Christ. After all, Christ was stripped of every dignity known to man to bring us into a right relationship with God. The point is that we no longer place a high value on all the accolades of worldly success. The attitude of the redeemed should always be: "If God wants to use my voice on social media, on my school campus, with my teammates or bandmates, then they are his to use. But they hold no value in comparison to knowing Jesus."

How is holding on to old things and following Jesus incompatible?

Paul went so far as to call all the things that used to be profitable to him dung. The point of using that word is to emphasize the word "loss." I think he makes his point. It is a radical attitude that seems logical only to those who value the prize of gaining and knowing Christ. The world isn't changed by those who spend their time and energy holding on to stuff; it is changed by those rare few who count everything as a loss to gain Christ. These individuals lead as disciples of Jesus.

> *Today, seek God's heart for what needs to be given up in your life. Don't look longingly at those old things you're letting go. Consider them loss and instead focus your heart on the only one you seek to gain—Jesus.*

DAY 4
FOUR QUESTIONS, ONE PURPOSE

"What is My Motivation?"

But one thing I do: Forgetting what is behind and reaching forward to what is ahead, I pursue as my goal the prize promised by God's heavenly call in Christ Jesus.
PHILIPPIANS 3:13b-14

It requires a singular and sacred motivation to influence a culture cluttered with the noise of competing worldviews. Those who make the most significant impact have the greatest of motivations. Motivation is one of those ideas that can be very difficult to define. The best definition I have ever heard comes from a book that would eventually become the play by Victor Hugo, *Les Misérables*. Sorry to all the Hamilton fans, but *Les Misérables* is at the top of my list for best play in theatre history. In the book, Hugo's character Cosette says, "To be lost in thought is not the be idle. There is visible work and invisible work."[3]

List three of the invisible motivations that absorb your thoughts?

Paul was a man "absorbed in thought" that heaven had reached out to him, and one day, he would reach heaven—the finish line of his race. This is why he used the phrase, "I pursue as my goal." It is an athletic phrase that would have stirred up the image of a Greek athlete running towards the finish line of a race. He was motivated by the idea that the reality of heaven awaited the end of his pilgrimage on earth.

In 1 Corinthians 9:24, he wrote, "Don't you know that the runners in a stadium all race, but only one receives the prize? Run in such a way to win the prize." Paul's invisible labor determined his visible labor.

How can things that no one sees lead to things that everyone sees?

Martin Luther, the monk who launched the Protestant Reformation movement, once wrote, "I have two days on my calendar: this day and that Day."[4] This day was referring to the present, but that Day referred to when he would step foot in heaven. I think the apostle Paul would have liked Luther's words. His motivation for the present moment seemed to be a future moment.

How can living for that unknown moment when you step into heaven impact how you live your life right now?

As citizens of heaven, we are gifted the greatest motivation in the history of the universe. Our invisible labor should be an excellent way for all that is visible in our life. The moment we will see Jesus face to face should determine everything about the moment at hand. One Bible translator interpreted Paul's statement this way: "Keep going on, trying to grasp that purpose for which Christ Jesus grasped me."[5] If we are rightly motivated, then our source of motivation will not weaken over time but rather only grow stronger with the birth of each morning.

> *As you close the week, pray that influencing others for Christ would be your invisible motivation for living.*

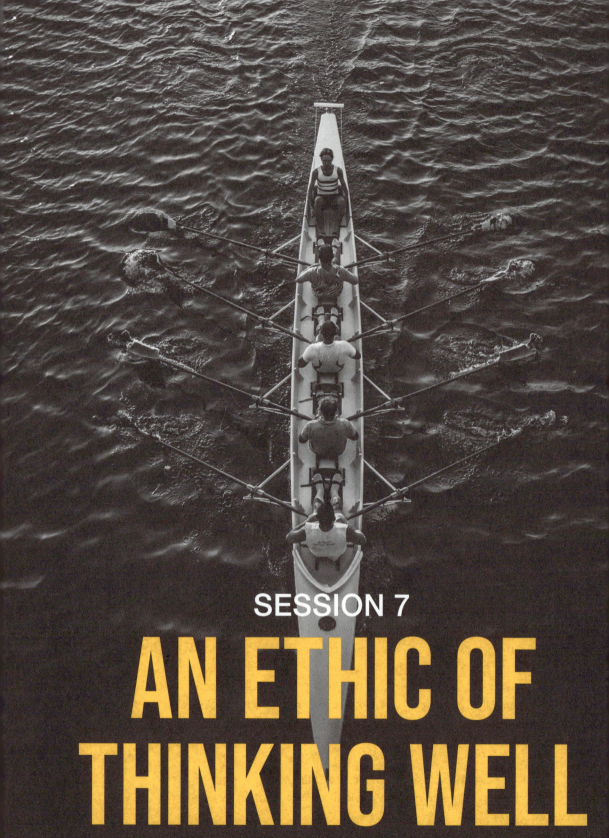

SESSION 7

AN ETHIC OF THINKING WELL

VIDEO GUIDE

INTERVIEW: Pat Williams

SCRIPTURE:

Finally brothers and sisters, whatever is true, whatever is honorable, whatever is just, whatever is pure, whatever is lovely, whatever is commendable—if there is any moral excellence and if there is anything praiseworthy—dwell on these things. Do what you have learned and received and heard from me, and seen in me, and the God of peace will be with you.
PHILIPPIANS 4:8-9

NOTES:

INTERESTING QUOTE:

KEY POINTS:

Abby and the Glowing Glass

Every morning Abby reluctantly rolls over to acknowledge the sound of her customized alarm. Depending on the day, she may tap the snooze button, but eventually she picks up her phone and embraces another morning. Before getting out of bed, thinking about what she may wear that day, or the tasks that follow, she stares into the glowing glass screen. It has become a daily routine to check for any missed messages and scroll through the latest social media posts before she starts her day. It's like Abby's morning coffee before her morning coffee. Updated on all that has transpired while she was sleeping, she is now ready to begin her day.

Like most of us who start our days staring into that little glowing glass screen, Abby will consume everything from the latest trends to tragic breaking news, all before getting out of bed. Throughout the day, she will post images to communicate her thoughts, chronicle her comings and goings in real-time, and continue to consume all sorts of content. Like the rest of us, she lives in an incredibly connected digital age—an age of extraordinary possibility that also carries with it the opportunity for destructive behavior.

At her church's midweek service, Abby listens to her youth pastor teach on 1 Corinthians 10:31, "So, whether you eat or drink, or whatever you do, do everything for the glory of God." Honestly, it's a verse she has heard referenced many times before. But on this occasion, the phrase "whatever you do" seemed to jump right off of the page. She had never given a ton of thought to her daily routine of swiping left, right, up, and down on that little glowing glass screen. It was simply the window to so much of her world. Abby wants to live her life for the glory of God, even when it comes to her phone, but she needs an understandable process that she can wrap her mind around to do so.

The Bible teaches us to "test all things" (1 Thess. 5:21). This verse could be phrased another way: "assume nothing." So how can we kick our assumptions to the curb and test or think well and wisely about such things as our online activity? Like Abby, many of us haven't given much thought to how we utilize social media platforms. Yet every day, we write another page in the narrative of our interactions and influence. To be intentional with our influence, we must be purposeful with the activity of our minds.

A RHYTHM OF REFLECTION

*Finally brothers and sisters, whatever is true, whatever is
honorable, whatever is just, whatever is pure, whatever is lovely,
whatever is commendable—if there is any moral excellence
and if there is anything praiseworthy—dwell on these things.
Do what you have learned and received and heard from me,
and seen in me, and the God of peace will be with you.*
PHILIPPIANS 4:8-9

What we think about is reflected in the manner in which we live our lives. It is a truth as old as time and taught throughout Scripture. Paul wrote in Romans 12:2, "Do not be conformed to this age, but be transformed by the renewing of your mind, so that you may discern what is the good, pleasing, and perfect will of God." The outward expression of transformation happens when there is a continual, inward renewal of our minds.

Take a quick poll to see what type of things people spend their time thinking about the most and try to piece together a top three.

Our minds are a passport that can lead down a path of holiness or wickedness. Paul wanted the church in Philippi to have the type of minds that were a gateway to holy living; minds that were filled with the peace of God. He wrote, "Do what you have learned and received and heard from me, and seen in me, and the God of peace will be with you" (Phil 4:9). So that they could live what they had learned and experience the peace that only God can give, he provided for them an ethic of thinking.

This system of Jesus-honoring ideas only works if they "dwell on these things" (v. 8). Paul taught that our minds and our thoughts must dwell on a Christ-honoring ethic of thinking if we are to live well and wisely. The word *dwell* means "a habit of thought that gives careful consideration and evaluation to a subject."[1] Careful reflection is a difficult task in a hyper-connected culture. The ability to detach from distractions in order to process a decision or issue has never been more challenging. Furthermore, creating a rhythm (or habit) of reflection is even more difficult. Nonetheless, it has never been more essential.

PHILIPPIANS

In order to create a rhythm of reflection—a continual space in our minds designed to help us consider and evaluate whatever we are facing—here are seven questions to guide our thoughts based on Philippians 4:8:

1. "Whatever is true" leads us to ask, "Am I allowing truth instead of others' opinions and cultural trends to frame my thinking?"
2. "Whatever is honorable" leads us to ask, "Could my thoughts be considered respectable? If my thoughts were made public, would they contribute or detract from a godly reputation?"
3. "Whatever is just" leads us to ask, "Am I thinking rightly about God and others? Am I giving them the justice they deserve?"
4. "Whatever is pure" leads us to ask, "Are my thoughts set apart and safeguarded from anything that is evil? Are my thoughts clean?"
5. "Whatever is lovely" leads us to ask, "Could my thinking be considered beautiful or attractive according to godliness?"
6. "Whatever is commendable" leads us to ask, "Are my thoughts proactively gracious and fit to be heard?"
7. "If there is any moral excellence and anything praiseworthy" leads us to ask, "Is my thinking and focus on that with moral value and worth celebrating?"

How could you remind yourself daily to run your thoughts through this seven question spectrum?

An ethic is awesome in theory but can be rather useless unless it becomes something you put into practice. It's like anything else, the more you practice it, the more comfortable you become with it. Eventually, this ethic of thinking will be a natural rhythm of how you mentally process life and its decisions. In others words, you can train your mind to think according to Philippians 4:8. How is this important as disciples learning to lead? Leaders are proactive. They take the initiative with their lives, and these seven questions enable us to be active, as opposed to passive, with the activity of our minds, especially our activity on those little glowing glass screens.

Discussion Questions

If you are supposed to dwell on "whatever is true," how do you know what is true?

If you are struggling with having only honorable thoughts, how can you root out dishonorable thoughts from your mind and heart?

List three ways you can strive to think justly and then live it out in your daily life.

How can your friends help you to think purely?

What are some things that inspire lovely thoughts in you? List three.

What are two thoughts you have that are worth celebrating?

Apply these question to how you use your phone. How would your activity change if these questions guided your online presence and interactions?

DAY 1
A CALL TO ACTION

Be a Leader Who is Known for Building Healthy Relationships

In this final week, let's do a thought experiment that will help us understand Philippians 4:9 from a different vantage point. What is transferable about Paul's leadership based on the following: "Do what you have learned, received, and heard from me and seen in me, and the God of peace will be with you."

The first observation is that Paul could ask them to practice what he had taught them and encourage them with his example because he had a relationship with the church in Philippi. As we saw in Session 1, the letter to the Philippians is in many ways a warm thank you note for the gift they had sent him and the love they had for him. Paul was a relational leader.

Who has been a relational leader in your life? What elements of his or her life are worthy to mimic?

One of the more neglected leadership skills is the willingness and ability to build healthy relationships. Whatever the reason for this neglect, Paul modeled that relationships are the vehicle for influence that stands the test of time.

How have you seen in your life that relationships lead to lasting influence?

This then begs the question, how do we become relational leaders? Here are four ways to begin:

1. Relational leaders value others' perspectives, voices, and talents.
2. Relational leaders demonstrate respect for others' contributions.
3. Relational leaders are uncompromising, fiercely optimistic, and protective.
4. Relational leaders confidently and proudly trust those they influence.

As you read over this list, how do you think these qualities help leaders build healthy relationships?

Building healthy relationships is as much an art form as it is a skill set. We don't build relationships to get influence; we build them because we believe in the present value and potential future of people.

Make of list of how you can practice the above characteristics of a relational leader. Here are some ideas of how to start: write some handwritten notes, serve, walk with someone and just listen, ask how you can help, befriend different types of people because you see value in everyone, and empower people to think, dream, and lead at the feet of Jesus. Energy spent investing in relationships is never wasted.

> *Ask God to help you have and build healthy relationships. Seek to put into practice the four tips to becoming a relational leader.*

DAY 2
A CALL TO ACTION

Be a Leader Who Shares God's Vision for Life with Others

Paul entrusted the Philippian believers to "do what you have learned and received and heard from me" (Phil. 4:9). What had they learned? What had they received? In short, a vision for God's desires in their church and city.

Those who followed Jesus in Philippi were given the opportunity to fulfill the desired will of God. Let that sink in for a few moments. God's vision for His creation—for His people—is clearly expressed in God's Word. The Bible is so much more than God's guide to moral living. If the Bible were only about moral living what a huge letdown that would be. It would feel so manufactured and human-focused. God has not given us the Bible so we could have a huge list of "do this" and "don't do that." It is far superior to moral living. You see, the Bible teaches how to live redeemed as citizens of heaven. Oh, the possibilities for living as a citizen of heaven on a problematic planet!

How is the Bible more than a handbook for moral living?

Disciples who decide to cultivate their influence to fulfill God's desires are in for an incredibly messy, unpredictable journey. They become the leaders who change the world by doing things others won't. For example:

- They look at a colossal problem and believe they can solve it.
- They don't speak the phrases, "it's never been done that way before" or "it's just too difficult."
- They aren't deterred by naysayers and people with the gift of cautioning others not to try.
- There is no divide too far, valley too deep, or mountain too high.
- They don't run from historical complications or cultural predicaments.
- They don't get distracted by trying to be picture perfect because their hearts rely on God's amazing grace.
- In a world where pain seems to have permanently moved into the neighborhood, they plant an eviction notice.
- In the shadows of consequence, they shine like stars.
- In the ashes of rejection and regret, they offer hope of a redeemed future.

Why? Because they are a living witness to God's good vision, and His vision is worth a lifetime of pursuit. His vision is worth sharing with others.

List three ways you can share God's vision for life with others today:

> *Pray that God would help you see His vision and that you would be willing to follow Him.*

DAY 3
A CALL TO ACTION

Be a Leader Who is an Example That Others Can Imitate

It cannot be stressed enough, avoid the very real danger of being the incongruent leader whose life isn't whole. Meaning the fictitious leader who says all the right things, but the content of their words is inconsistent with the character of their life. Instead, always aspire to be the leader who is the teacher that embodies the teachings. Harmony between message and messenger is the hallmark of authentic leadership.

Have you ever encountered someone who said the right things but didn't live them out? What type of influence did this person have?

For a long time, when I read Paul's words in 1 Corinthians 11:1, "Imitate me, as I also imitate Christ," I couldn't help but feel a bit confused. I'd think, *I can imitate Christ on my own, thank you very much. And by the way, Mr. Apostle-man, Jesus walked on the seashore of my life and said, "follow me," not "follow Paul as he follows me."*

But the longer I have followed Jesus, the more I have awakened to the reality that Paul wasn't calling me to follow him after all. Instead, he was saying that the imitable quality he possessed was that there was consistency between his life and his beliefs. In mimicking this element of Paul's life, I could imitate him without fear of failure. I could imitate him without the baggage of pride and opinions, without worrying about getting exposed as a fraud, pits to fall into or stumbling blocks to trip over. If there is symmetry between what I say and what I do, I don't have to worry because I'm being authentic and real in everything I do.

How does living out what we say free us up to be imitated as well?

The journey Paul was on felt in some unexplainable way like both of our homes—because together we are imitating the one who has called us "citizens of heaven" (Phil. 1:27). In fact, it has become my goal to live in such a way that if someone were to imitate me, they wouldn't even know it. Instead, they would feel as though they had arrived at a place for which they were always intended. A place they would simply know felt right—like home.

Read Hebrews 13:14. How does this verse help you understand the concept of "home" described in the previous paragraph?

In recent years there have been far too many stories of leaders who led double lives. They were individuals whom we trusted and admired, and since they have fallen, our trust has been broken. It has become difficult not to look at other leaders and think: "I wonder if they too have a closet full of skeletons?" You nor I can change the past, and there may not be a lot we can change in the immediate moment. But we can live a life that embodies our beliefs. A life that is harmonious and consistent. A life that is worth imitating.

> *Today, pray that your life would be harmonious, both in word and deed. Then take some time to pray for leaders you know and love to have the same harmony in their lives as well.*

DAY 4
A CALL TO ACTION

Be a Leader Who Emphasizes God as the Hero of the Story

Paul was a relational leader who shared with Philippi God's desires and even served as a spiritual role model. The great benefit they received from his teaching and by following his example was embodied by Philippians 4:9: "the God of peace will be with you." As followers of Jesus, as citizens of heaven, it is easy to think that the only reward is the promise of heaven. But Paul wanted them to know that as you pursue heaven, you will discover that the God of heaven pursues you. He had already explained to them, "the peace of God, which surpasses all understanding, will guard your hearts and minds in Christ Jesus" (4:7). Now he wanted them to know that the peace of God and the God of peace was with them.

Describe a time when you felt the peace of God with you.

From a leadership perspective, Paul models for us an all-important truth: God is the hero of the story. While this may sound simple, I assure you it is quite countercultural. It's an obvious reality that we live in a world where everyone wants you to know their profile name and where being an influencer, trendsetter, or going viral seems just within our digital reach. We all tell a story with our actions, posts, and interactions. Every story has a central theme, characters, plot, setting, and conflict. The challenge in our leadership story is this: to tell a story that has redemption as the main theme and the Redeemer as the hero.

Look over your social media posts from the past week. Who is the hero in your posts? What is the main theme of your posts? Be honest.

Life is short; it's like a fog that dissipates when the morning light touches it (James 4:14). But it is also a beautifully magnificent opportunity to tell a story; one that will impact others and can reverberate for generations to come. A story that leads others to walk with the God of peace. It is a fascinating idea that while life on this earth is short, we can tell a story in it that will help others in turn tell their stories. It is even more remarkable to think that just one story can change the world.

Write out three ways you can leverage your social media presence to tell the life changing story of Jesus to a watching world.

In the end, all we can do is tell our story. It is our offering back to God who so richly blessed our lives with Jesus. So, let your story shine with the light and love of Jesus. And let it be said that yours was a story worth telling, an example worth following.

> *As you close this Bible study, reflect for a few uninterrupted moments on the story of Jesus. Then pray that God would empower you to live in the truth of that story and influence others to know that story for themselves.*

PHILIPPIANS
LEADER GUIDE

NOTE TO LEADER: Thank you for agreeing to lead this study. Helping students grow in their influence is not only of great benefit to them, but it helps grow and build up the church. Remember, you don't have to be perfect to lead a group; just be willing to love students by being available and genuine with them. So, pray up, prepare, encourage freely, lead by example, and be willing to adjust as you grow together as a group.

SESSION 1: The Art of Initiative and Gratitude

WELCOME: Welcome students who have come to be part of this study. Make sure everyone knows each others' names before you begin (including you).

WATCH: Watch the Session 1 video together. Encourage students to use page 7 to help them take notes and follow along.

DISCUSS: Use the material found on pages 8-11 to lead a discussion on the session. Take advantage of the discussion questions on page 11.

APPLY: Each week an application activity will be provided to help students begin to practice leading in the areas the session covered.

CREATING A WARM WELCOME
This activity requires some items to be gathered in advance: poster board, magic markers, glitter, colored pencils, scissors, stencils, and so on. As a group compile a "gratitude" list. Use words or phrases that encourage and edify like, "I'm thankful you're here," "you matter," or simply "Welcome!" Using the poster board, ask students to paint, draw, or stencil these words or phrase on the paper. Once everyone is finished, strategically hang or place the words and phrases around the room. The point of this exercise is to create a warm welcome, and by doing this, we begin to practice a crucial part of Paul's leadership.

> Close in prayer. Be sure to write down students' prayer requests each week that you meet. Check in during the week to let them know you are thinking of them and praying for their needs.

SESSION 2: The Excellent, Bold, Optimistic Leader

WELCOME: Greet each student as they arrive. Call them by name and review names if necessary. Briefly review Session 1 and ask students what stood out to them from their personal study.

WATCH: Watch the Session 2 video together. Encourage students to use page 21 to help them take notes and follow along.

DISCUSS: Use the material found on pages 22-25 to lead a discussion on the session. Take advantage of the discussion questions on page 25.

APPLY: Provide pens and paper for each student and walk them through the following steps.

HOW LEADERS THINK ABOUT PROBLEMS
STEP 1: Write down three to five real world problems that presently exist in our world. Are any of these causing divide among Christians?

STEP 2: Zero in on one problem and discuss and identify factors that have contributed to the problem. Are there historical factors? Are there technological factors, such as social media or other digital platforms? Are there political factors? Has polarization contributed to or created the problem?

STEP 3: Discuss one way to creatively think about solutions and lead through these challenges as followers of Jesus. Remember, the answers to problems in a broken world must follow the redemptive path demonstrated for us in the session. Any solutions must be born out of a growing love. Answers that are born out of a growing love are worth being boldly and unashamedly shared. Leaders must possess the divine perspective that we have identified as optimism. The leader's optimism will help others have hope and endure until resolution to the problem has been achieved.

> *Close in prayer. Follow up with prayer requests from last week and write down any new requests students may have. Check in during the week to let them know you are thinking of them and praying for their needs.*

SESSION 3: Humility

WELCOME: Greet each student by name as they arrive. Briefly review Session 2 and ask students what stood out to them from their personal study.

WATCH: Watch the Session 3 video together. Encourage students to use page 35 to help them take notes and follow along.

DISCUSS: Use the material found on pages 36-39 to lead a discussion on the session. Take advantage of the discussion questions on page 39.

APPLY: Provide pens and paper for each student and walk them through the following steps.

CONSIDER OTHERS FIRST

STEP 1: Direct students to get into groups of five or six people. Each person will need a piece of paper and something to write with.

STEP 2: Within their groups, challenge students to take a few moments to write down three characteristics they admire about the person on their left. Ask for a volunteer to begin and go in a clockwise motion, allowing each person to share one or more characteristics that they respect and admire about the person next to them.

STEP 3: Write down a healthy memory you have with someone else in the room. Recall a time when that person made you feel heard, known, and/or valued. In no particular order, invite those who feel comfortable to share the memory with the group. (Note: allow students to share a memory between anyone in the room, not just those in their circle.)

> *Close in prayer. Follow up with prayer requests and write down any new requests students may have. Check in during the week to let them know you are thinking of them and praying for their needs.*

SESSION 4: Countercultural Success

WELCOME: Greet each student by name as they arrive. Briefly review Session 3 and ask students what stood out to them from their personal study.

WATCH: Watch the Session 4 video together. Encourage students to use page 49 to help them take notes and follow along.

DISCUSS: Use the material found on pages 50-53 to lead a discussion on the session. Take advantage of the discussion questions on page 53.

APPLY: Buy or make a gold star badge for each student in your group.

GOLD STAR

Before your weekly meeting, write a personal note to each student reminding them that they are to illuminate the darkness of this world by accomplishing God's good purposes. In your note, encourage each student to define leadership success according to their response to God's desires. As you pass out the notes, remind students that Jesus desires to work in and through them. In order to do this, we must seek to live a "blameless and pure" life so that we might shine like stars in the world and show people the hope we have in Jesus (Phil. 2:15).

> *Close in prayer. Follow up with prayer requests and write down any new requests students may have. Check in during the week to let them know you are thinking of them and praying for their needs.*

SESSION 5: Empowerment

WELCOME: Greet each student by name as they arrive. Briefly review Session 4 and ask students what stood out to them from their personal study.

WATCH: Watch the Session 5 video together. Encourage students to use page 63 to help them take notes and follow along.

DISCUSS: Use the material found on pages 64-67 to lead a discussion on the session. Take advantage of the discussion questions on page 67.

APPLY: Each person will need five note cards and a pen or pencil.

THE REALLY SIMPLE, SLIGHTLY ELEMENTARY, POSSIBLY SENTIMENTAL, GAME OF APPRECIATING EMPOWERMENT

STEP 1: Write the name of a person that has empowered you to "go on in the name of God" on one side of each note card. On the opposite side, write out how that person has empowered you using one of the ways Paul demonstrated his belief in Timothy (see p. 66).

STEP 2: Place all the cards in one container and mix them up. Take turns drawing names and read out loud the description of empowerment before turning the card over to read the name. If they choose, allow the person who wrote the card to offer further explanation for their card, such as the story of how the leader empowered them. The game has two objectives: First, to highlight practical ways that empowerment is already taking place. Second, to edify and encourage those leaders who have invested their time and energy in empowering someone else.

> *Close in prayer. Follow up with prayer requests and write down any new requests students may have. Check in during the week to let them know you are thinking of them and praying for their needs.*

SESSION 6: The Myth of Confidence

WELCOME: Greet each student by name as they arrive. Briefly review Session 5 and ask students what stood out to them from their personal study.

WATCH: Watch the Session 6 video together. Encourage students to use page 77 to help them take notes and follow along.

DISCUSS: Use the material found on pages 78-81 to lead a discussion on the session. Take advantage of the discussion questions on page 81.

APPLY: Each person will need a piece of paper and a pen or pencil.

FROM RÉSUMÉ TO REASON

STEP 1: Give each student a piece of paper and ask them to create a personal résumé. Instruct them to include details about their family, schoolwork, and any accomplishments they may have achieved (sports, music, theater, work, etc.).

STEP 2: Beside each element, ask them to write one way God can use these things for His purposes. Even if some of your story has been challenging (parents' divorce, bad grades, getting cut from the team, etc.), consider how God might bring reason from that hardship.

STEP 3: Ask for volunteers to share how God can use them for His purposes through the things they are involved in and have experienced. Encourage students to see that even though Paul couldn't lean on his résumé anymore, God used him and gave him a reason in spite of the things in his past.

> *Close in prayer. Follow up with prayer requests and write down any new requests students may have. Check in during the week to let them know you are thinking of them and praying for their needs.*

SESSION 7: An Ethic of Thinking Well

WELCOME: Greet each student by name as they arrive. Thank them for being part of the group and for sticking with it to the end. Briefly review Session 6 and ask students what stood out to them from their personal study and any lasting impressions they will take from this study moving forward.

WATCH: Watch the Session 7 video together. Encourage students to use page 91 to help them take notes and follow along.

DISCUSS: Use the material found on pages 92-95 to lead a discussion on the session. Take advantage of the discussion questions on page 95.

APPLY: Each person will need a piece of paper and a pen or pencil.

THE ACTION THAT WILL RESULT FROM THINKING

STEP 1: Identify an activity or type of decision that you typically complete without much thought and write it down. Underneath, number one through seven along the left side of the page.

STEP 2: Answer Yes or No to each of the seven questions from page 94 to the activity or decision.

STEP 3: Write out an action that will result from your answers to Step 2.

STEP 4: Altogether or in smaller groups, spend some time discussing the answers to each question and the action that will result from that thinking. The point of this step is to have a conversation. Allow others to respond, challenge, or simply ask questions about how thoughts were formulated and turned into action. There are three simple rules for Step 4: Be graceful. Be patient. Allow for some measure of disagreement.

> *Close in prayer. Follow up with prayer requests and pray a blessing over the students in the group as this study comes to an end.*

END NOTES

SESSION 1

1. Robert Fulghum, *All I Really Need to Know I Learned in Kindergarten: Uncommon Thoughts on Common Things* (New York: Ballantine Books, 2003) 36.
2. Fulghum, 37.
3. The phrase "the Practice of the Presence of God" originates with Nicolas Herman (1614-1691, who would come to be referred to as Brother Lawrence of the Resurrection).
4. *It's a Wonderful Life*, directed by Frank Capra (1947; Culver City, CA: Liberty Films).
5. M.R. Vincent, *The Word Studies in the New Testament*, vol. 1 (New York: Charles Scribner's Sons, 1887), 731.
6. W.W. Wiersbe, *The Bible Exposition Commentary*, vol. 2 (Wheaton, IL: Victor Books, 1996), 343.

SESSION 3

1. K.S. Wuest, *Wuest's Word Studies from the Greek New Testament for the English Reader*, vol. 5 (Grand Rapids: Eerdmans, 1997), 59.

SESSION 4

1. James M. Kouzes and Barry Z. Posner, *The Leadership Challenge: How to Make Extraordinary Things Happen in Organizations*, 6th ed. (Hoboken, NJ: Wiley, 2017) 18-20.

SESSION 5

1. P.L. Tan, *Encyclopedia of 7700 Illustrations: A Treasury of Illustrations, Anecdotes, Facts and Quotations for Pastors, Teachers, and Christian Workers* (Garland, TX: Bible Communications, 1996), e-book, 916.
2. Tan, 916.
3. Francis Gerald Ensley, *John Wesley: Evangelist* (Nashville, TN: Methodist Evangelistic Materials, 1958), 7.
4. Tan, 916.
5. *Selected Letters of John Wesley,* ed. Frederick C. Gill (New York, NY: Philosophical Library, 1956), 237.
6. Wuest, 82.
7. J. P. Louw and E. A. Nida, *Greek-English Lexicon of the New Testament: Based on Semantic Domains*, 2nd ed., vol. 1 (New York: United Bible Societies, 1996), 447.
8. Louw, 409.

SESSION 6

1. Rick Reilly, "Life of Reilly," *ESPN* [online], 23 December 2008, [accessed 1 June 2021]. Available from the Internet: https://www.espn.com/espn/rickreilly/news/story?id=3789373.
2. Reilly.
3. Victor Hugo, *Les Misérables* (New York: Penguin Group, 2013), 470.
4. Lewis Guest, "This Day and That Day: The Pressures of Today and the Returning King," *Desiring God* [online], 25 September 2020, [accessed 1 June 2021]. Available from the Internet: https://www.desiringgod.org/articles/this-day-and-that-day.
5. J.B. Phillips, *New Testament in Modern English* (New York: Touchstone, 1972), 415.

SESSION 7

1. A.T. Robertson, *Word Pictures in the New Testament* (Nashville: Broadman, 1933).

Get the most from your study.

Customize your Bible study time with a guided experience.

As disciples of Jesus, we have been given the great responsibility of stewarding our influence for the glory of God. We were created to think, dream, and lead at the feet of Jesus. Leadership is, then, cultivated under the overarching purpose of discipleship. This is why leadership doesn't begin with action, but rather identity—not with what we can accomplish, but rather what Jesus has accomplished for us. In this study we will dive into Paul's letter to the first church ever planted in Europe. A closer look allows us to glean the transformational ideas that successful leaders have embraced, both past and present.

In this 7-session Bible study, we will learn from Student Leadership University Vice President, Brent Crowe, as he examines the life and leadership of the apostle Paul, exploring key elements of Christ-honoring leadership.

To enrich your study experience, we recommend purchasing the accompanying *Philippians* video teaching sessions. Each video session includes an interview with a different Christian leader in 15-20 minutes of invaluable learning and encouragement for students.

Brent Crowe's teaching sessions are available for purchase or rent at lifeway.com/philippians.

ADDITIONAL RESOURCES

PHILIPPIANS GROUP VIDEO BUNDLE
Session videos with author Brent Crowe interviewing Christian leaders

PHILIPPIANS TEEN BIBLE STUDY EBOOK
A 7-session study on learning to lead as a disciple of Christ